J JACKSON BENTLEY

with

RICK & NIKKI COCHRANE

THE COLLECTED **RIXFLIX** SHORT STORIES

The Heritage Collection

fidus

fidus

©J Jackson Bentley 2023

All rights reserved.
Without limiting the rights under copyright reserved above,
no reproduction, copy or transmission of this publication may be made without written permission of both the copyright owner and the publisher
of this book.

~

This Heritage Edition published by www.FidusPress.com in the UK & USA 2023

Fidus Books is an imprint of:

The Fidus Press
Chorley. England. UK

~

This is a work of fiction. Names, characters, places and incidents are either the product of the author's imagination or are used fictitiously, and any resemblance to actual persons, living or dead, or to actual events is entirely coincidental.

~

Kindle edition is set in Calibri 10 & Candara 12

INTRODUCTION TO THE SERIES

Having watched Rick and Nikki on RixFlix from their humble beginnings I would show their vlogs on our large screen 4K TV to my wife, who suffers from Multiple Myeloma They entertained her throughout her tough cancer treatment and then through shielding during the Covid lockdown for almost five months. Her happy place was Orlando and RixFlix brought it into our home every day.

I broached the possibility of a book based on RixFlix with Rick and Nikki at a chance meeting at Universal and, eventually, a quadrilogy unfolded. Along with Rick and Nikki I also have a great fun relationship with Miss America, Labby the Cabby, Murph at Chez Alcatraz and others.

It has been fun writing thriller short stories about real people and mixing it in with my other writing commitments, it has also given me an opportunity to return to my comedic roots, I was a comedy writer before I wrote anything else.

I travel the world as an author and as a legal consultant, 39 countries to date, and am a very lucky man. So when I began writing fiction, I donated all of my royalties to charitable and other worthy causes, hoping that I might sell a thousand or so copies. Well, we have now sold well over two million copies and our chosen charities have welcomed the cash.

Life may be short or long, but it is all the more pleasurable when we meet diverse people, create long lasting friendships and sacrifice for the wellbeing of one another. Read long and prosper.

J. Jackson Bentley

A Message from Rick and Nikki, to you.

What can we say, we love to share our adventures and misadventures with our viewers and listeners. As a result, our channel has grown exponentially in a relatively short time.

Our household and lives are consumed with RixFlix and Rick's Roadtrips, and now with reading fictional books about our exciting lives.

Our marriage and family are our stability, we are just an ordinary couple with extraordinary opportunities. We meet so many unbelievable people as we film and livestream. It is impossible to imagine how we would hear so many wonderful life stories if you did not follow us, stop us to talk and write to us.

Of course, we constantly need to work hard to find subscribers to keep the show on the road, but the rich blessings we have encountered since starting on this journey have been innumerable.

Now that the kids are grown, we have more kids - you all. We always look forward to meeting and speaking with you and converting a passing meeting into a lasting friendship.

We are grateful to you all and especially to JJB who makes us laugh with his British wit and who is committed, with his lovely wife, to helping us ensure that RixFlix is a success on both sides of the Atlantic.

Do we like being terrorised in short stories, its fine, the books are funny, and they allow Rick and myself to let you into our lives via amusing stories and fictional antics.

This collectible edition is for you.

Rix Flix   *Nikki*

Dedication and Autograph Page

Our thanks to everyone who supports RixFlix, bring us your copy of the book and we will personalize it for you. See if you can collect the signatures of Rick, Nikki, JJB, Murph and others from the books.

Original Cover Art

J JACKSON BENTLEY
ZERO DAYS WITHOUT INCIDENT

A RixFlix Short Story

Copyright J Jackson Bentley/RixFlix 2022

Published by Fidus USA
An imprint of www.FidusPress.com

All rights reserved. This is a work of fiction. Real world places, characters, and companies are re-imagined and used in a fictitious setting throughout this story. No similarity to actual real-life characteristics, actions or behaviours is intended.

The cooperation and permissions of Rix Flix and its named owners, subscribers and followers is appreciated and applauded by the author. All proceeds to supporting Rix Flix and Road trips Channels.

Visit www.MyRixflix.com and Watch Rix Flix on You Tube.

In this Short Story the shenanigans begin when a shield representing Gryffindor is affixed to the wall of the RixFlix Studio. Gryffindor is represented by a Lion.

Original Authors Note:

In 2016 I was in Busan, South Korea on business when my attention was drawn to an article in an English Language newspaper. The article concerned a brilliant engineering science student at a University in Seoul who was expected to produce a practical working solution to a real-world problem for his Masters' Degree.

It seems he chose to produce a web slinging device - yes, as per *The Amazing Spiderman!* The device was designed to effectively, and safely, disable an assailant carrying a weapon. The sticky web would confound the assassin and glue their weapon to their hand.

In the demonstration it worked reasonably well. The web was fired from the oversized barrel and the sticky web, constructed from fine carbon fibre veins coated with heated adhesive, bound the weapon to the hand and the hand to the body.

When it came to remove the web once it had cooled and set, the student experienced rather less success. The unfortunate mock assailant had to attend hospital, where the sticky web was removed over a period of hours with the liberal application of solvents. The volunteer had red blotches on his skin for the remainder of the semester.

This series of stories is a departure for me as a thriller writer, it was written for the entertainment of that group of individuals who love and follow RixFlix. Any money raised will be used to support the RixFlix channels, neither Fidus nor myself will accept any revenue or payment. So, enjoy, subscribe to RixFlix, and become a producer, let's all keep the Universal ball rolling.

JJB/January 2022.

"…..nothing is done in this world that is not witnessed by a camera of one kind or another."

Excerpt from The US Congressional Record August 4th 2021.

PREFACE

Mountain to Sea Trail, Durham, North Carolina. USA.

Dominic could feel the cold kiss of the north wind chilling his neck. The snow beneath his sodden feet was fresh and deep; it had fallen quickly, and it had taken him by surprise. He had chosen the spot for disposal with the utmost care a week ago. In the winter months this off-trail path was usually deserted, especially early in the morning.

When he had initially reconnoitred the area, he found many large fallen trees covered with dark green moss, teeming with hungry insects. There were also deep crevasses that housed all manner of hungry scavengers. Close by there were small caves that still bore the remnants of summer campfires. These caves were little more than rocky overhangs really, but they offered shelter from the summer rain. Today, in the snow, they were virtually inaccessible.

Without the snow the body would have lain undiscovered for weeks, by which time Dominic would have been long gone, and the forest animals and other critters would have eaten their fill.

Unfortunately, with a body in the back of the old Jeep Cherokee, bought anonymously at an estate sale, Dom did not have the luxury of being able to wait for a thaw. Hence the perilous depositing of Hayley Truett, former spinster of these parts, in less-than-ideal conditions.

He deposited the body closer to the road than he would have liked. He pushed it under a fallen tree trunk and covered it with loose snow, using the blanket in which her naked body had been concealed, to dust the virgin snow over the compressed and footprint ridden snow beneath. It could never be perfect, but at worst the body would be found when the snow melted. And that would not be until the weak winter sunshine penetrated this deeply into the wilderness, weeks from now.

Luckily, Dominic had chiselled the carving on the tree on his last visit to save time today. The Chinese symbol, depicting the number four, was obvious and apparent to anyone who looked. He never carved the symbols into a tree too close to the body; after all, the police and FBI deserved a challenge.

***

By the time Dominic arrived back at the road after his disposal of the girl's remains, it was beginning to fill with cars. He should have guessed. A hill that would have probably remained deserted for months during a cold damp winter became an instant tourist destination when the snow fell. Cars, well wrapped-up kids, and excited adults decanted from vehicles of all kinds carrying snow boards, tin trays, old advertising boards, anything that would slide down the snowy hill at murderous speed.

Dominic exited the forest about a hundred metres from his recently acquired vehicle. He had become disoriented in the woods and could not retrace his earlier tracks. As he looked towards the vehicle, he spotted a man leaning on the old white Cherokee with a phone to his ear. His heart beating rapidly, and with perspiration misting his brow, Dominic approached the man as casually as he could.

The man ended the call as he saw Dominic approach, smiling.

"Broken down, friend?" Dominic asked, looking first at the car and then at the man. The man smiled back and relaxed. Dom lied. "I have jump leads in my Ranger!"

The man shook his head as he responded.

"No, man, I'm fine, my own car is back along the road. My wife, brother and kids have gone sledding, but I noticed this." He pointed at a thin blood trail consisting of tiny drops that would have gone unnoticed on any other day. But today the tiny red droplets shone like neon from the pristine white snow.

"Damn it. How could I have been so careless?" Dom demanded of himself silently. The other man continued.

"The car has been here awhile. Look, it has a layer of fresh snow," the man said as he ran a finger across the hood. "I was thinking the driver might have been hurt, and so went looking for help while it was still dark." He stopped speaking and gestured at the wintry vista surrounding them. "But there is nothing around here for miles. The driver may be lying injured somewhere in there." He looked pointedly into the lightly wooded forest, the trees skeletal and bare, stripped of their summer clothes.

"Are the emergency services on their way?" Dominic asked, thinking on his feet.

"Yep. Fifteen minutes out," the man replied. Dom had an idea.

"Look, neither of us are heroes but someone might be lying just yards away, injured and unable to call out. What say we follow the blood spots, just for a hundred yards or so, and see what we find."

The man looked hesitant.

"We could be saving a life!" Dom prompted. That did the trick. The man looked at his watch. "We'll give it five minutes, then we come back and wait for the authorities."

Dom nodded. "Agreed." He only needed five minutes.

***

The kindly man had neither seen nor expected the blow to the back of his head, as he took the lead in following the bloody trail. He would wake up woozy in a few minutes with a mild concussion and a bump on his head, courtesy of the heavy bone handle of Dom's hunting knife.

Back in the old Cherokee, driving quickly away from the scene, Dominic became aware that these roads had been left largely untreated, which made them hazardous, especially on the downhill stretches. But he needed to get away now. He could not dawdle. He must not return to the cheap apartment he had been renting in Durham. It was essential that he get as far away as possible, as quickly as possible.

He had been driving for just a few minutes when a 'Police' emblazoned Dodge Charger, decked out in black and white, passed on the other side of the road, sirens blazing. Dom was relieved when it passed by.

His relief did not last long. The police car spun and immediately began pursuing the white Cherokee, Dom's tags matching those on the laptop computer between the front seats. It seemed that the man now lying unconscious in the woods, had given a very detailed description of Dominic's car when he called 911.

***

The super charged Police Dodge was a great asset on dry roads, but it was no faster than the Cherokee on icy terrain. Nevertheless, with the aid of some expert driving, the Charger was gradually narrowing the gap, and Dom became nervous, he knew that police cars seldom hunted alone. They were pack animals.

Just ahead of the Cherokee lay a tight bend. Dominic could see the dull sheen of the ice on the untreated road, but what could he do? If the car left the road it would slide into a deep, snow filled trench, but at least he would be largely uninjured. Then he had an idea.

***

The police driver had trained for these conditions and was confident that they would apprehend the Cherokee driver at the next straight, flat piece of road, just a mile ahead.

He closed on the Cherokee just before the bend, hoping to force the driver into an error, perhaps into an icy spin, thus halting the chase and keeping the sledding enthusiasts heading up the hill safe from a reckless driver.

He was just yards behind the Cherokee when it did something unexpected. It braked hard on an icy road.

***

The Cherokee fishtailed as soon as Dominic jumped on the brakes, then it began a spin. A spin that was arrested when the Police Charger slammed into the back quarter on the passenger side, straightening the Cherokee up again.

The Charger inevitably suffered more damage than the heavy structural steel frame of the old Cherokee, and its front offside wheel assembly collapsed. The police car entered an uncontrolled skid, launching into the air and landing in the deep trench designed to prevent cars rolling down the hill.

There was a loud crash, then silence. The sirens and lights went out. The Police car was now largely buried by snow.

"Florida," Dom thought. "Now there's a state with no snow and a host of lonely unattached people."

He kept driving.

***

A rookie Patrolman was the first officer to spot the abandoned Jeep Cherokee the next day. It was parked close to the Raleigh Union Station. A station with a regular Auto Car Train Service to Sanford, near Orlando, and Disney World – where dreams come true. Dom had his own dreams, but they usually resulted in the worst kind of nightmare for those he befriended.

Collectibles

Rick had anticipated that Nikki, his long-suffering wife, would be at work when the box was delivered. He was wrong. It was a 'snow day', and his schoolteacher wife was enjoying a midweek day at home.

For the uninformed, the term 'snow day' is used loosely in Central Florida. Simply stated, some school administrators decided that they had no real need of an efficient heating system, and so the District Supervisors agreed ludicrously high rates for heating power with their supplier, to secure lower bills for the much-needed air conditioning. Such was the punitive pricing schedule agreed for heating power that, should a school with this agreement then deign to use the heating on a cold day, even for a morning, the power company executives would be found celebrating their prospective bonuses with champagne and cigars before lunchtime.

In Central Florida it was often simpler to just cancel school on the coldest days and thus maintain the school district power budgets. So it was that a 'snow day' had been declared when the TV weather on the 'ones' announced that a frost could be expected in some areas. True to form, the weather dipped into the forties Fahrenheit in the early hours of the morning and the decision appeared wise. It appeared less wise when the lucky "snow day" kids were spotted outside playing in their Disney tee shirts by 10:30am, by which time the temperature hit 67 degrees Fahrenheit.

As a result, Nikki was at home, editing videos, her workstation in plain sight of the curb side where any package delivery van would park.

***

Far from Rick's home in Winter Park, on the other side of Kissimmee, and a few miles away from the theme parks, was the attractive sounding "Sunshine Pines Resort", a trailer park that had not only seen better days, but it had also probably seen better centuries. This park did not attract visitors or tourists, it housed those who could not, or would not, afford a more permanent and adequate dwelling.

The occupancy turnover rate at Sunshine Pines was akin to that of a cheap long stay motel whose owner was constantly shouting at his elderly mother, poor old Mrs Bates! In truth, most of the residents moved out at night, actually in the early hours of the morning, so as not to be seen leaving by the landlord.

However, none of this deterred Dominic Cleary from renting a 32-foot long - wide twin, with potential for a hot tub connection. He was happy being an anonymous man, part of a forgotten community.

Dominic had been raised in a deeply religious household and had all of the requisite skills of a homemaker; his mother had made sure of that. Dominic had a good degree and a decent masters from a Mid-West University. He was living here from choice, not from necessity.

The modest trailer home was neat, clean and tidy. The furniture was worn but comfortable and the utilities worked just fine. Occupying the unit closest to the mains, he found that the water pressure was especially powerful, just what he needed, in fact. He had a lot of blood to wash out of his working clothes tonight.

***

The brown UPS truck rolled up outside the house at 11am and the driver leapt out of the ever-open door to retrieve Rick's parcel from the back. Rick wondered why UPS and the US Postal Service bothered buying their Florida vehicles with doors, as they were rarely used.

The driver lifted a large cardboard box off the corrugated bed of the boxy van and looked up at the sky. Perhaps he was expecting rain, or a comet hurling earthwards; either seemed just as likely given the cloudless blue sky above.

Rick ran to the door.

As soon as the front door of the house closed behind the delivery man, who had insisted on taking a picture of Rick holding the box as proof of delivery, Nikki shouted out a question.

"What's that."

"It's a box."

"I meant what is in it?" she responded.

"I don't know, I haven't opened it."

Suspicious at the lack of a direct answer, Nikki was by Rick's side by the time he set the box down on the table.

"Well, it's not for me. So, I am assuming you have an idea of what is inside," Nikki commented, and then continued. "Or do we need to call the bomb squad?"

Rick frowned. "It's just something than came up on eBay, I didn't think it would be of interest to you."

Nikki was now more curious than ever. "I have heard that some *special* deliveries are made to men of a certain age in plain brown packages," she smiled, but Rick didn't notice. He was looking intently at the box.

"I have to say I am offended by the implication that...." He didn't get to finish the sentence. Nikki cut in.

"Just open the box Rick, I'm going nowhere."

The plain brown box was opened and gave way to a smaller box sealed in cellophane and kept in place with inflated plastic packing balloons. Rick lifted the inner box out of its secure packaging, and it became clear that this was a toy of some kind.

The packaging was bright blue and red, and the design followed a spider's web theme. The web design was photo realistic and a seemingly three dimensional. Spiderman appeared to be pulling aside the web and trying to escape the flat box.

The box simply read, Web Slinger, and the name of the toy was repeated below in Chinese:

网络花环

"You've bought a children's toy?" Nikki stated not realising the serious error she was making, or seemingly fully considering her poor choice of words. Rick was quick to correct his wife, a lesson he had not learned in over two decades of marriage. He did so with conviction and not a little disappointment in his voice.

"This is not a toy; it is a rare collectible. It's a feat of engineering, and it fires real webs."

His pitch made, he lifted the box to examine it closely, holding it at eye level with a reverence reminiscent of the Maji presenting presents to the baby Jesus in ancient Israel.

Nikki sighed and returned to her editing. Rick considered an unboxing video, but could not wait, and began to peel away the shrink-wrapped plastic, the first layer of many.

The cardboard box was ingeniously designed to have no obvious point of entry. The Taiwanese were clearly a cunning race. Rick rotated the box through 360 degrees more than once, looking for a tab to pull or flap to open. Eventually he found a plastic security tab which he cut with a craft knife. Still the box remained stubbornly closed.

Not wishing to destroy the box, Rick teased it open a millimetre at a time until the glossy box revealed its secret, another plain brown box inside.

After ten more minutes the contents were spread across the desk ready for assembly, along with the craft knife, a steak knife, a pair of scissors and a pair of pliers with wire cutting facility (for the plastic zip ties holding the web slinger to its glossy cardboard display).

Rick was sweating from the exertion of it all, whilst Nikki was sitting at the computer just shaking her head. Her long blonde hair was flattened to the side of her head by the noise reduction headphones she had resorted to when Rick's grumbling about the box turned into a rant about overly complex packaging, Chinese puzzle boxes, and their role in the inevitable fall of the Ming Dynasty.

Nikki knew that Rick would have a wonderful hour or two trying to assemble the *collectible* Web Slinger, then he would give up and read the assembly instructions. His afternoon was spoken for.

***

Across town at Sunshine Pines Resort, Dominic Cleary had cleaned the trailer and sanitised his working clothes. As he sat down on the well-worn sofa, he closed his eyes and recalled the exquisite moment he despatched his latest victim to the next world.

Lorraine Dewey had been a dental hygienist. Dominic liked professionals; they were so eloquent in their final pleas for mercy. She had initially succumbed to his charms when he had magically turned up beside her with an open umbrella just as a typical Florida downpour began. It was like an unapologetically romantic scene from Breakfast at Tiffany's, in her mind. In an instant she was Audrey Hepburn and Dominic was George Peppard.

Back in the real world, Lorraine had been far enough from shelter that she would have been soaked to the skin by the time she reached safety. Dominic just smiled and guided her to an awning, where he neatly folded the umbrella before courteously introducing himself.

"Hello, my name's Dominic. I thought you looked as though you needed rescuing." His face was that of a film star, perhaps from a Hallmark Christmas Movie rather than a blockbuster, but his eyes... they were blue-grey, shot through with dark speckles. They seemed to expose his very soul.

Luckily for him they did no such thing. They concealed his soul and hid his intent. It would take a strong woman to resist his charms when he was laying them out, and Lorraine was not that woman. She didn't just feel weak at the knees, she felt weak at her core.

"Let me get you a coffee. We'll shelter inside until the rain eases." Dominic took her gently by the elbow and led her into Starbuck's. He still had the cups on his trophy shelf, their handwritten names inexpertly scribed in felt tip pen by the Barista, 'Dom' and 'Loz. They were collectibles.

Great Power Brings Great Responsibility

With Nikki back at school and the latest vlog uploaded to YouTube, Rick had some time on his hands before his midweek trip to the Theme Parks.

He carefully unwrapped the assembled Web Slinger and breathed in its new toy odour as he caressed its retro high impact plastic case. The engineering prowess used to create this collectible gun was truly exquisite.

Spiderman, the original Peter Parker, had always fascinated Rick. He was still young – as was Rick at the time. He had problems – didn't we all? And he sometimes allowed his frustrations to overcome his sense of duty, something we could all admit to, surely. Rick read the comics and watched the animated TV series that espoused the inevitable truth that Spider Man could do anything a Spider can, spinning webs of any size to catch crooks just like flies.

Rick ran the old song through his head, but his mind kept leaping to the mock choral version often played in Springfield as he toured Universal Studios. The tune was the same, but the refrain was "Spider Pig, Spider Pig, does whatever a Spider Pig does!" Silly but catchy.

Following the operating instructions, and not just because the warning, in sixteen languages, was printed in bold, but because he wanted the Web Slinger to work so much, he carefully assembled the components. First the webs. They were constructed of fine veins of interlocking carbon fibre, all splaying out from a weighted centre, like rays of the sun. The re-usable webs were loaded into a small disposable cartridge that was contained in a large magazine that would take six such cartridges. On the press of the trigger, a CO^2 capsule would fire the cartridge along the oversized barrel, about an inch in diameter, until it achieved optimum speed.

At the end of the barrel there was a steel ring that stopped the cartridge in its tracks before dropping the empty casing to the floor. The web then continued its journey outside the barrel at high speed. At first it was packed like a parachute, or folded umbrella, with the weighted centre taking the projectile into the open air and in the direction of its target.

As it travelled, normal gravitational and centrifugal forces opened the web, so that when it arrived at its destination it would be fully open, and ready to ensnare any crook, just like a fly.

The thing that made the gun special were the two small canisters on either side of the gun. These each contained a single component of a two-part resin that had to be mixed to become sticky, thus preventing the unfortunate thug from untangling themselves from the web.

The mixing of the two chemicals took place at the end of the barrel just as the web was released into the air. On its own each component fluid was inert, but together, they rocked!

The very liquid sticky residue, now in the form of a fine mist, dispensed via a spray nozzle. The adhesive mist would adhere to the web as it was ejected. Then, as the web travelled, the chemical reaction would warm the mixing chemicals, create the new compound and sail towards its target. As it travelled further, the residue would cool and become tacky, making it adhere to any surface. Rick could hardly wait tr try it.

***

Dominic's web was of a very different construction. His was a web of deceit, a neatly – and well-practiced – story entirely fabricated within the confines of his twisted mind.

After three dates Lorraine Dewey was trapped in his web. She did not realise it and she did not care. Dom was the man she had waited for her whole life.

Dom looked at the sweet girl. He imagined that he could see exactly what she had looked like as a child. Her slightly rounded face was pretty, but in a childish way, not beautiful in the classic sense. She had slightly overdone her make-up; her eyes were dark and had the appearance of being drawn by an artist. Dom also wondered what skin condition might be concealed below the heavy layer of golden bronze foundation. He would find out later.

As Dom relived the night with perfect recollection, he sighed. In his mind's eye he had just arrived at the moment he cherished in every such assignation - the moment of realisation. The terror dancing behind the wide eyes of the victim when they knew that kissing was soon to turn to killing.

Lorraine was braver than she had appeared. She fought. She would not beg for her life, even when she was restrained and subdued. As she was subjected to each new horror, she would sob at first, but then that defiance would take over once again and she would fight.

Dom rewarded her grit by allowing her to survive almost twice as long as his previous three victims.

***

With no evil villains in the neighbourhood, or mad Doctors with eight tentacles threatening his friends, Rick had to find a target. In the end he settled for a blank space on the newly decorated wall of the video studio, the den.

Aiming carefully to avoid accidents - all too common when he was experimenting or being too enthusiastic on a road trip - he fired.

There was a satisfying hiss as the CO^2 did its work. The cylinders completed their task silently, and the sticky web flew across the room in a perfect arc, landing as an open web exactly where he had aimed.

Rick was in heaven. It was Nirvana. He had dreamt of such a moment from being a boy. He just sat and looked at the perfect spider web on the wall. Its silvery colour contrasted nicely with the flat pale green emulsion paint that Nikki had spent her entire weekend applying sometime around Labour Day the previous year.

After admiring his handiwork for several minutes, including snapping several pictures on his iPhone 12, Rick decided that Nikki was unlikely to appreciate the beauty of the web as much as he did, or respect it as much as it richly deserved. So, he would take it down, remove any sticky residue and no-one would be the wiser.

At least that was the plan.

***

Lorraine was tucked up neatly in the storage space behind the back seat of the old Ford Bronco. The Bronco was the original shape, emanating from well before the Ford designers had resurrected it as a charmless Korean style 4x4.

Dominic climbed in and took the old vehicle across unmade ground and into an area of woodland that was as well known for fly tipping as it was for hunting.

He laid Lorraine's naked body out on the forest floor, discreetly covering her with branches and leaves to maintain her modesty - she would appreciate that, Dom imagined.

As he left the scene and returned to his car, Dominic took a few moments to carve an icon into the bark of a tree. When finished, he looked at his handiwork; it showed a Chinese character:

五

The ruthless killer was a great lover of the winter Olympics, and the Chinese character would undoubtedly confuse the local police. Perhaps someone clever enough would work out exactly why the killer had carved the number 5 on a tree, and then his fame would grow as hapless law enforcement officers across the country suddenly realised what they had missed.

***

Rick was due to begin a Live Steam video in just over ninety minutes and the web on the wall has set hard. Nothing would move it. There was no way on this sweet earth that Nikki would be amused by the web or find it to be a welcome addition to their décor. The web had to be gone by the time school was over.

After trying a few more products and yet more tools, the web stubbornly clung to the wall. There was only one chance, only one man he could turn to. Rick reluctantly turned to Gordon, the elderly retiree next door. A man who could talk for the USA in the boring conversations event and win a gold medal.

Ten minutes later Gordon Trent stood at Rick's side looking at the web.

"That ain't coming off easily," the grey-haired neighbour noted uselessly. "Just open my toolbox, please. Then pass me the aerosol can with the hazard notices on the front."

Rick picked out the can which, rather suspiciously, had no branding and very little explanation of its contents. It looked industrial. It looked as though it might have a serious use in a factory setting. It also carried a warning. "Danger! Used in confined spaces this product may cause breathing difficulties and, in certain circumstances, cause death."

Gordon noticed the horror on Rick's face and spoke calmly. "They have to say that to cover themselves. It's as safe as houses. I used it in the Army, in bomb disposal, all the time."

***

It was Gordon's opinion that the sticky substance holding the web onto the wall was a two-part epoxy resin that had been designed to create a non-setting compound. Unfortunately, the mix had failed, and it had hardened. It could be removed with solvents, but the wall finish would inevitably be ruined in the process and the drywall might have to be replaced.

Rick groaned.

Either he trusted an old man with a toxic spray, or he had a hole in the drywall. He was doomed. The livestream was now an hour away.

Grabbing his bag, he slipped on his yellow Nike shoes and spoke to Gordon. "I have to go to make my final appearance on YouTube while still possessing all of my body parts. Do what you can."

Gordon grinned widely. It was the first time in three years that Rick had seen the old man smile.

Rick groaned again.

***

Fifteen minutes later, and racing against the clock, Rick left Gordon and the web, hoping that the old man was not quite as mad as he appeared.

As he drove Rick felt a glimmer of hope as the sunshine warmed him through the windscreen of the Jeep. Gordon's hazardous spray had frozen the web solid and left it brittle. Reassuringly, Gordon had already painstakingly chipped away a quarter of the outer extremes of the web without damaging the paintwork.

An unexpected optimism had started to penetrate the fog of fear. This might end well after all. Rick began to believe that he may just get through the day without a visit to the Emergency Room.

And if Gordon failed? Then surely over twenty years of marriage had to count for something. Didn't it?

That Fellow in Yellow

The livestream was going well. It had begun on time and people around the world were tuning in to see what was happening at Universal Studios today.

The camera really does lie. It was chilly in the park and Rick had resorted to a long sleeve tee to accommodate the weather, but to the viewers it appeared to be a warm, sunny and cloudless day. As usual Rick was wearing a yellow cap that determined his allegiance to Hufflepuff House at Hogwarts and a yellow Ron Jon shirt that gave a hint at his surfer boy past. His yellow Nikes completed the look, with only the cargo shorts not complying. The cargo shorts were not a fashion statement, they were intended to break up the solid yellow look and discourage unruly kids from yelling 'Banana Man' from a safe distance.

Rick set the camera down, or as he announced to his live streamers, he was setting the 'Kids' down for a moment. He was dehydrated; he needed a drink from the Chez Alcatraz booth. A young woman provided him with a plastic cup of chilled water at his request, free of charge.

"Hey Murph!" Rick called out to the senior bartender. The man looked around but seemingly did not see Rick. Obviously, it was impossible not to see a six-foot man of stature dressed in yellow not six feet away. Nonetheless, Rick was obliged to wave to attract Murph's attention. It worked.

"Sorry Rick, didn't see you there in those camouflage pants, you blended right into the background."

Rick looked down at his shorts before realising that Murph was playfully mocking him.

"So, when are we going shark diving, then?" Rick asked. In a moment of weakness Murph had apparently agreed to accompany Rick on a shark diving trip. Just the divers, the open waters and hungry sharks. Madness. Murph liked imitating a shark, as he served drinks with a rubber glove puppet, squirting copious amounts of red liquid into a pale blue long drink that represented the sea but encountering one in the water sounded less enjoyable.

Murph was, quite reasonably, concerned at offering his nicely rounded torso to one of natures most accomplished killers, but he figured he would be safe. After all, if they lost a few tourists every trip, surely word would get around.

Additionally, having customers eaten by sharks would be a notoriously poor business model in terms of repeat customers. Unless the sharks just took a limb or two. Even then you could imagine what a deterrent that would be to returning customers:

"Hey fella, I admire your determination coming shark diving with just one leg. It must be harder to swim."

The one-legged customer standing in line may reply, "Well, I actually lost my leg here on my first trip, six months ago. I did complain but the captain said that the shark was just being playful. He told me that if Jawsy had been serious, I would have really been in trouble." The one-legged man would then laugh manically and almost fall off his crutch.

Murph's mini daydream ended, and he returned to reality. He had a plan to survive shark diving with Rick. He would train. He didn't need to be faster than a shark, just faster than Rick!

***

Back at the house, Gordon admired his handiwork. The web was gone but there were five bare patches where the centre of the web had proved to be more resilient.

The elderly neighbour looked around and his eye alighted on a large coat of arms for Gryffindor House, just sitting on the floor. "That'll do the job", he thought as he reached for his hammer and a picture pin.

***

Rick posed for the last of today's pictures with two young women from Delaware who were wearing yellow Minions sweatshirts.

"You're taller than you look on TV," one of the girls remarked with a twinkle in her eye. It was a comment Rick heard regularly. Rick laughed off the flirtatious remark. Nikki was editing this later and he was in enough trouble already.

***

Nikki was at home when Rick returned. Thankfully Gordon was long gone. In fact, when Rick pulled up in the Jeep, Gordon had pulled aside his own window blinds and given Rick the thumbs up. Rick relaxed and felt a wave of relief wash over him. He could settle down and watch Jeopardy without being in it.

When he found Nikki, she was at the computer in the den. Rick immediately glanced at the offended piece of wall. It was clear of marks or damage. He breathed out; he hadn't realised that he had been holding his breath. However, a new piece of Potter memorabilia had appeared on the wall where the offending web had so recently resided. To Gordon's credit, the polished walnut shield that held the house logo looked right at home. It was placed centrally on the wall and looked to be a deliberate decorator choice.

He wondered whether Nikki had noticed. He did not have to wonder for long.

"Thanks for putting up the shield. I was wondering where we should put it. It looks quite good there." She paused. "Although, I was thinking over on the far wall between the door and the wall." She pushed the wheeled office chair back as if she was going to stand and try the shield in its alternative location.

Rick deliberately blocked her way, as casually as he could, and said:

"Let's leave it there for a week or two, see how it goes. If we don't like it, we can move it then!"

Nikki turned back to the monitor and said, "Good idea."

Perp Search

It was four days later, and Dominic felt dreadful. He had cold symptoms, his bones ached, his muscles complained, and his head hurt. He couldn't taste a thing.

Two tests and a doctor visit confirmed that he had Covid 19, despite two vaccine jabs. He had been in his bed twenty hours a day for two days already, and he feared it may still last a few more. Nonetheless, he had the internet, the TV and YouTube for entertainment. He could lie on his side, best for breathing but not so good for his aching hip, and watch Fox decimate President Biden, CNN cry sedition, and all manner of weird people advocate for their own mad cause.

In amongst it all he could watch lighter programming on YouTube, videos of people in theme parks, repairing old cars, searching old barns for treasure, and his favourite, True Crime Vlogs.

His own crimes had not yet been covered on YouTube, which was both a relief and a disappointment, but he felt sure that in time his meticulous and murderous workmanship would come to light.

In fact, when the doctor had asked him from whom he had contracted the virus, he had felt a burning desire to say, "A girl called Lorraine, but don't worry about tracing her, she's dead." Instead, he just smiled and said it could have been anyone.

***

Nikki arrived home at the prescribed time but with a visitor, Mrs Hemmings, a grey-haired retiree who had, until recently, taught at Nikki's school. Rick once had a third-grade teacher called Mrs Hemmings who had terrorised him, and everyone else probably. Even the Principal and the school supervisor were afraid of her, he recalled – possibly erroneously. This lady looked very much like his Mrs Hemmings.

She did not bump his offered fist but looked sternly at it and shook her head. Rick offered his hand instead, and she shook it firmly. When she released it, Rick unobtrusively pushed the bones of his right hand back where they should be and smiled. "Welcome to our home."

Mrs Hemmings turned out to be a gentle soul deep down. Very deep down in Rick's mind, she was a woman with an obsession. The old teacher claimed to be a True Crime afficionado (her term).

In the 1980's she had written a few pieces for a True Crime magazine which was characterised by garish comic book style covers showing buxom women in unlikely cleavage revealing outfits being assaulted or threatened by a thin man, often with a moustache.

Then in the late 1990's she started a True Crime online message board, where people could dial in to the world wide web and contribute their opinions on potential culprits in less than and hundred words.

The 2000's brought a True Crime Blog and in 2017 a YouTube Channel where the followers tried to solve crimes and track down the villains using the power of the crowd.

Nikki explained the nature of the older lady's visit. "Annalise wants someone to take over the weekly vlog. It reaches an average of eighty thousand viewers, has over twenty thousand subscribers and four hundred active supporters who donate to the upkeep of the channel."

Whilst Rick was sceptical, he knew that Nikki was a detective by nature; at least she had found him out on every single occasion he did something wrong in twenty years of wedded bliss. His reluctance was driven by a desire to keep things light.

Nonetheless, the three of them talked for a couple of hours and agreed that Nikki and Rick would take over the channel, at least for the time being. Mrs Hemmings was going to Europe for a prolonged trip. She joked that she would return with a new husband, her own having been at peace for over a decade. Blissful peace, Rick thought uncharitably.

And so began a new adventure, *PerpSearch*, a crime blog for those who like to solve a puzzle and who like to pursue criminals online, from at least three states away.

***

Dominic was feeling miserable, sickly, locked away in his self-imposed exile in a trailer park in Florida. He was becoming depressed. He had set himself a goal of ten victims before returning to his own pampered life, back in California, but that was now looking unlikely.

His mission had begun three months ago, just a few days after the tragic death of his mother, the one woman on this earth he had been capable of loving. Of course, he felt affection for other women, even lust, but not love. In his teenage years he had crushes, passions and testosterone fuelled desires, the same as any young man. But, despite his looks, pristine personal hygiene and his apparent good taste in clothes, girls failed to appreciate him enough to go on more than two or three dates. His aunt had explained to him that he came across a little too keen.

Later in life he attended University, taking additional lessons, electives, in interpersonal relationships and there he quickly discovered what he had been doing wrong all those years. He recognised now that he had been exuding desperation. He appeared intense, needy and was far too quick to attend to the needs, or wants, of the girls he was dating. It seems they too preferred subtle meta messages, a little tension and the thrill of the hunt.

Once he had obtained the key to attraction, he set the principles he had learned to work, and work they did. He practiced the tactics that he had learned in psychology classes, developed strategies for each different relationship, and exploited them ruthlessly.

Soon, relationships that would have taken months or years to develop naturally were cynically fast tracked by Dominic. The women he chose as subjects for his experiments were still reeling from one romantic gesture or liaison that when the next appeared, they were almost breathless. He generated the heady romantic excitement girls had read about in magazines, but which had seemed unattainable, and which in reality were unattainable. At least at such speed.

His first victim was Calley Frost, the young and single fashion designer from Palo Alto who had been texting on her phone when her Toyota 4Runner collided with Dom's mother's smaller compact car. Dom's Mom died at the scene, whilst an unhurt and unfeeling Calley Frost complained to a police officer that she needed to get to an important business meeting.

Dom buried his mother and then determined to avenge her.

Where There's Trouble, There's a Scoop!

Nikki was home alone. Rick was out, having dinner with his mother. When the doorbell sounded, she checked the monitor before opening the door. There was a policeman standing on the doorstep. She opened the door quickly. Policemen appearing unexpected at your door was rarely a good thing.

He showed his ID and asked if he could step inside. Nikki noticed that the young man was driving his personal vehicle.

The young man called her by her full name before asking, "May I call you Nikki? I have seen your videos so many times it seems odd calling you anything else." Nikki nodded her assent and they sat down opposite one another, Nikki sitting on the couch, the officer in an armchair.

"There is nothing to worry about, Nikki." The young man began. "I'm here because my aunt is Annalise Hemmings."

"Is she OK?" Nikki asked, concern in her voice.

"Oh, yes, she's fine. She asked me to call on you and explain something." Nikki looked puzzled and so he continued. "I have always been Aunt Annie's source for her crime vlog and when I went to her with my latest tip, she referred me to you." He paused. "I have to say it feels wrong going outside the family on something like this, but she assured me that you and Rick were rock solid reliable." He looked to Nikki for confirmation, and she smiled.

"Nothing we hear from you goes any further unless we discuss it first."

Officer Ray Dalton relaxed and sank back in the armchair. He had been perched nervously on its edge. Once he was comfortable, he began to open up and tell his story.

"I have spoken to Rick a few times now at Universal. I often get the gig there on Tuesday mornings and Wednesday afternoons." He was referring to the fact that Orlando area police officers were assigned duty inside the parks every day.

"I'm sure that you heard about the sad case of Lorraine Dewey, the girl found dead in woodland at the edge of the state park."

Nikki nodded. It had been on every news outlet for a week. The girl was found naked and disfigured, but the police kept the rest of the details to themselves.

"Well, Nikki, she bore no signs of sexual molestation or internal damage, that much was reported in the Metro section of the Sentinel, and so I'm giving away no secrets. However, I was the second car on the scene, and I was assigned to secure the crime scene when the detectives showed up. In doing so I saw something odd, something I thought might be relevant to the enquiry. I reported it to the detectives, who dismissed my concerns but who ordered the crime scene techs to take pictures anyway.

As it was, and still is, outside the crime scene perimeter, I have no concerns about sharing the photo with you." He took out his phone and tapped a few times before turning the phone to Nikki.

Nikki prepared herself for the worst, but when she looked all she saw was a carving in the bark of a tree trunk. It looked like a Chinese character, and everyone was familiar with those now that it was two weeks into the winter Olympics in Beijing.

"I checked the image on Google Image search at the time and on many occasions since. It is the simplified Chinese symbol for the number 5."

He paused.

"No-one in the police is going to alarm the public on the basis of a carving on a tree fifty yards away from a dead body, but Nikki, I think we might have a serial killer in the locality."

***

The next day Nikki and Rick stood in the woods overlooking the crime scene. Strands of crime scene tape remained but there was little to see. Rick chose not to video the scene out of respect for the victim. He did, however, video the tree and its carving.

"How is it that the police are not taking this seriously?" Nikki asked.

"Maybe they are. It's possible they're looking for the four other incidents as we speak." Rick was always optimistic.

In fact, the police had a local man in their sights, a man known locally as JoJo, a homeless man who lived in a shelter in the woods in the winter, and who had a record of violent assault. Albeit the assaults had always been related to trespassers on his adopted plot of land.

JoJo was being sought actively and, until he was found and excluded from their enquiries, that is where the local police efforts would be directed.

***

Rick and Nikki were still in the woods discussing where to go for lunch when a grating voice yelled in their direction. They turned to look. A dark figure stood in the shadows, silhouetted by the light shining into the open field behind them.

They couldn't make out who the person was, or even their gender. What they saw quite clearly, however, was the shotgun, and it was pointed directly at them.

Everybody Needs an Origin Story

There is no doubt that Dominic's first killing was less controlled and measured than killings two to five. There was a residual anger at the woman whose recklessness took his mother's life and resentment for the authorities who punished the woman in such an off handed manner. She did not receive a custodial sentence, nor did she lose her licence forever; she lost her license for twelve months and accepted a suspended sentence.

Dominic had been abroad at a conference at the time of the hearing, or he would have made his victim statement in person. He could hear his father's words ringing in his head "Don't get mad, get even." Then he would hear his mother saying, "forgiveness is the only way to find peace."

The words of his errant and often absent father prevailed.

Calley Frost had suffered over a period of three days before being unceremoniously dumped in the desert. The Chinese symbol for the number 1 was scratched into a nearby rock.

Why Chinese? No reason. He just wanted to throw the police off his own trail. It didn't work, of course. Within a day of finding the body of his first victim, two detectives turned up at his house early in the morning.

They informed him that Ms Frost was dead. He said nothing. They explained that she had been murdered. He said nothing. They postulated a theory that someone who lost their mother to a callous and reckless driver might seek revenge, by way of killing the driver. He invited them in.

It was clear from their expressions that they had rarely been in a house so large in this expensive area of LA, or a house so exquisitely decorated. They admired his artwork as they moved slowly into the recessed lounge area that housed a wraparound leather sofa that would have seated a dozen guests.

Dominic, not the name he was using then, flipped open his new Galaxy foldable phone and scrolled down the screen.

"Let me see if we can bring this interview to a swift close, so that you can pursue the real killer of this odious woman. Not that she deserves justice when she escaped it so easily. Tell me, when was she killed?"

"Actually, we ask the questions," the older detective noted.

"And you will be asking them of my lawyers for the next three months, should I choose to exercise my rights. I am trying to assist you here. Please don't be obstructive. We are doing so well."

Remembering who they were addressing and having little confidence that a man of his standing would stoop to murder, they answered.

"It is estimated that she was killed on Friday night, between 10pm and 5am Saturday morning. Her body was dumped where it was found, probably Saturday night.

The crime scene technicians, the pathologist and a soil scientist have all reached similar conclusions."

"Well, it seems your journey out into the Hills today was worthwhile. I can save you some time. I was in Vegas for a conference on Friday, Saturday I stayed on and swam, took in a show and had dinner with a friend. Sunday, I drove back."

"Can you confirm all of this, sir?" The second detective asked.

"Of course. I will have my secretary email you with my receipts, the names and numbers of my colleagues. Oh, and the contact number of my dinner companion."

The detectives wanted everything there and then, but when you were interviewing a prospective candidate for Governor someday, you trod carefully.

Dominic, real name Carswell Lawrence Judd, smiled as he waved off the unmarked black Crown Victoria. He had covered all of his bases. There were few people in his circle who did not owe him a favour, their loyalty or their job. Yet more were keen to have him keep their secrets.

It was amazing what he had learned about the rich and famous in his rise from junior partner at a law firm to Deputy Attorney General of the Great State of California.

As he stood at the door and watched the police car drive away, he pondered on the question that would set him on a crusade, a cruel and wicked crusade.

"If I can escape justice so easily after killing a woman so closely linked to me, I wonder how many women I could kill when my relationship to them was unknown?"

***

"What exactly are you two doing on my land?" It was a woman's voice and as she walked towards them, they relaxed. They could now see a genteel countrywoman in tweeds. She looked down at the shotgun.

"Oops. Sorry about that," she said, breaking the shotgun and rendering it harmless. "I was pursuing a fox, a vixen actually. I feel a bit sorry for her, truth be told. She and her little family are probably hungry to the point of starvation. But I can't let them fill up on my chickens. They are a rare breed and I love them like I love my dogs."

The old woman examined Rick and Nicky with a weathered eye and decided that they looked like good folks. "Well, I am Jane Fannon, the landowner here. Now who might you be? Introduce yourselves."

***

Rick and Nikki told the story of how they came to be on her land and in return she explained the discovery of the body, the aftermath and the seemingly casual approach of the police.

"They weren't even interested in my CCTV." Nikki had worked for women like Jane. They did not like to be answered back to but most of all they could not forgive that greatest of all sins, the ignoring of them or their views.

"I gave the police a copy of the CCTV footage, but they weren't too keen. A very junior officer called me three days later and thanked me but said that it had not been helpful." She harrumphed as if they had failed her, the murdered girl and the world at large.

Thirty minutes later they were driving away in the Jeep with a copy of the CCTV footage on a USB stick, and words of Jane Fannon ringing in their ears.

"I don't care what the police say about a crime of passion or a local homeless man being responsible, this was something else. It was an act of sublime cruelty." She paused. "And you have to be unbalanced to harm any poor girl in that way."

Rumour Alert, Rumour Alert!

Dominic Cleary had been the name of a good friend of Carswell Judd. The unfortunate man had been an officer in the Marines and had served in Afghanistan, and in other countries he took care not to disclose. He had seen death at close hand and had probably taken the lives of enemies of the United States, again at close hand. He bore the unhealing scars that came from taking the life of another and his bent shoulders carried the unbearable burden of his past.

When he died in a motel room in Montana, Carswell was at his side. Carswell had received a call from his distressed friend and travelled across two states to save his old friend from doing something stupid. He was too late.

As soon as Dominic saw Carswell's Lexus turning into the motel car park, he injected himself and lay on the bed. Dominic died an hour later from that deliberate overdose, whilst gripping Carswell's hand the whole time and not letting him seek help.

Everything Dominic had, the little that he possessed, he left to his friend. Carswell had a company take care of the legal formalities and he paid for the man's cremation.

Without really understanding why, he kept all of his friend's identification papers, passport and documents.

***

Rick pulled the backcloth tighter as Nikki clipped it to the aluminium frame. They stood back and admired their handiwork. Rick had been a little annoyed when Nikki insisted on referring to the instructions when the frame was clearly easy to erect. When it was completed, he had to admit it was nice to build something just once for a change, albeit that admission was never made vocally.

With the camera situated in its usual place the result on the screen was wonderful. To all intents and purposes, it would appear to the subscribers that they were broadcasting from a law library. In fact, just inches behind the backcloth were their usual Disney and Harry Potter collectibles, along with Rick's prized Shrek 4D glasses.

They were about to rehearse their lines, as if that really ever happened, when Nikki said, "You know, I'm going to move that house shield to the other wall." She stood and made a move towards the shield and its hidden secrets.

"I can do it later," Rick said as he too stood, towering over his wife. Then a note of resignation entered his voice. "You already know, don't you?"

Nikki looked stern. "I knew from the moment I walked in that day. I assume it was the Spidey weapon." Rick nodded. "I was just waiting to see how long it would take to get an admission from you." She looked at him, trying not to laugh at his discomfiture.

"It's not as if I didn't leave you clues!" She added. Rick looked puzzled. Nikki continued. "I reset the "*Days without incident* notice to zero, on that first day, and I have adjusted it every day since."

The days without incident poster was a joke that they used in their broadcasts to liven up their updates with funny stories about their, mostly Rick's, mishaps. It was so commonplace that Rick saw it every day without really noticing it.

Nikki laughed. "Don't go planning anything for the weekend. You have a wall to paint." Actually, she had been unhappy with that shade of paint ever since it dried darker than expected after being applied, but it wouldn't hurt to be less than completely honest, just this once.

***

Dominic decided that he would call it a day on his deadly mission, even though he had set a shocking target of ten women. After all, he could always take up his ghoulish hobby at some future date. For now, he had to consider packing up and returning to California. He had a career to reignite.

When last year's Gubernatorial contest had been lost by his boss and close political ally, they were both shattered. Don, his boss, said that he would not run again; he believed he was too old.

So, it would be Carswell Lawrence Judd who would make a run in four years' time. Unfortunately, the next few months of bureaucratic re-organisation would be painful for him and so he approached the new Governor with a request for medical leave for the fully mandated period of three months. It was granted on the grounds of his heartbreak and the mental health impact of his mother's unexpected death.

The three months were up, and whilst no-one in the new administration was pushing him to return, he knew he must return and rebuild if he was to run for Governor next time around.

He would leave his rented trailer, unregistered vehicle and Florida behind in a week's time. Or so he thought.

***

The first true crime vlog had gone well. Obviously, there were a few fluffs, but overall, it was editable.

As they wrapped up the first episode Rick flashed up a picture of the Chinese symbol carved into the tree.

"Now, we are not saying with absolute certainty that this is related to the crime, but it was in the vicinity, and it had been carved recently. Worryingly, the symbol represents the number five." He paused for effect. "Which might make you wonder whether there are four more symbols, and four more bodies out there somewhere." He spread his arms to indicate the potential spread of these crimes across North America. Nikki moved her head back just in time to avoid a big hand connecting with her nose. There was very nearly an 'incident' in episode 1. Rick continued to speak without acknowledging the situation.

"This week Nikki will be chasing up a lead from a Californian blogger who is sending us a picture of another Chinese symbol, this one representing the number one, which was found very close to the scene of a murder out there in the desert. Are they related?" Rick inclined his head and mumbled, "Who knows?" Suggesting, of course, that he was sceptical. "Press the subscribe button and the bell, and when the next episode of *PerpSearch* is ready you will be the first to know. But please don't miss it because we have exclusive video from the most recent crime scene. After seeing it maybe you, our followers, can solve this crime, or help the police to track down the perpetrator.

Until next week, 'Be good, or be careful.'

The Man Behind the Mask

Dominic looked very different to the dapper and perfectly groomed Carswell Judd. The Assistant AG wore only the sharpest Italian suits, shoes from London and his hair was cut and styled by Giorgio every week at The Hollywood Salon just off Rodeo Drive. In between times expensive hair products made sure that not a hair strayed from its place, whilst looking as though no effort at all had been made to achieve the look.

When Carswell looked in the mirror, he could easily imagine a younger Rob Lowe staring back at him. The characteristics he adopted for Dominic were almost the polar opposite.

Carswell could not bring himself to reduce his hygiene regime, but he could allow his hair to grow out and then cut it himself before applying supermarket own brand gel. His beard was left largely unkempt and had been showing the first signs of grey hair.

The images of the two men did not lead one to the conclusion that they were the same man, or even related. They shared the same dark hair and that was the end of the similarity for most casual onlookers.

***

Dominic had been enjoying the *PerpSearch* video channel until now. Where did they get these crazy vlog names?

Rick and Nikki were co-ordinated in specially designed tee shirts adorned with a cartoon picture of themselves above a faded graphic of the Blues Brothers' police cruiser and the words "We're on a Mission". They looked like a fun couple; he would hate to have to kill them.

He especially liked the fact that they suggested a serial killer was out there and that somewhere three bodies had not been connected to the man the media would come to call the *Symbol Slayer*, in their usual understated way.

He was about to close the page down when he heard the fateful words "... in the next episode we have exclusive video from the most recent crime scene."

That brief, innocent sounding phrase changed everything. Rick and Nikki had progressed from being True Crime Vloggers to potential True Crime Victims.

Follow the Yellow Rick Road

Rick had announced a Midweek Mania live cast, as usual, from Universal Orlando. He would be at that park around noon and would begin broadcasting soon thereafter. It was anticipated that he had planned to spend most of his time in Islands of Adventure, inasmuch as he ever had a plan.

Dominic was already there, but he had his own agenda. The man was barely recognisable. He had attempted to bleach his hair blond, but the result was closer to ginger. No matter, it was different.

After the *PerpSearch* video he had realised that whilst he had mostly worn a Covid 19 medical mask when he deposited the body in the woods, he had removed it to sit down and take a breather, to suck in cool fresh air. If some crazy wildlife afficionado had placed a Go Cam or some other tiny camera in the woods to catch sight of a rare Albino Crested Cardinal, or some such critter, he might have been inadvertently caught on camera.

Back in the day, before he was Dominic, he had appeared on CNN, CNBC and even Good Morning America regularly as Carswell Judd, and whilst he looked very different today, if video of him in the woods was broadcast widely enough, someone would be sure to recognise him.

The police had kept the video quiet, if they had it, and he needed to make sure that Rick did, too. Whatever that took.

***

Rick arrived as planned at Valet Parking and, after a little banter about having left his firearms at home, he headed off to security. The valet checked around the car for existing damage and then headed into the control booth to hang the keys.

Dominic casually strode over to the cars awaiting transfer to the garage and opened the white Jeep's door. The weather was still cool enough for Rick to keep the Jeep's doors on. The serial killer then wedged a burner phone loaded with a tracking app under the seat, closed the door and casually followed the yellow shirted vlogger into Citywalk, always maintaining a safe distance.

***

For the next two hours Dominic shadowed Rick as he traversed Islands of Adventure, chatting to livestreamers and park guests as he went. If Dom lost sight of the six-foot yellow shirted vlogger, no problem. He just tuned into the livestream broadcast on his phone, and he could see where Rick had been a minute or so ago.

Dom caught up with Rick as he chatted with friends beside Poseidon's Fury. The ride was closed but outside the hoarding were cast members dressed as archaeologists, intent on entertaining the crowd. Rick and his friend were their only visitors at present. He listened to the banter.

Rick's friend, referred to only as JJ, was clearly English. The man spoke with a regional accent that Dom could not identify but which was not a typical London dialect.

"This is my friend Rick," the man said, obviously familiar with the actors. The three actors said hello to Rick's camera. Then one of the actors said to Rick directly, "You may have read my book – Archaeology through the ages."

Before Rick could respond his friend interjected with: "Only if it had lots of pictures." There was laughter all around at Rick's expense.

"I have a copy of your archaeology book," the English friend said. "I keep it on the shelf next to my copy of 'President Biden: Master of Memory' and President Trump's book on '101 convincing comb overs."

There was silence all around as people stifled guffaws. Only Dom laughed out loud. It was a reasonable joke but in today's culture, political satire could get you cancelled.

Eventually Rick separated from his followers and headed back to valet parking, with Dom in close proximity.

***

Dom lost sight of the white Jeep Wrangler almost as soon as it departed the Valet Parking lot. He was caught at a red light. Three sets of lights later the Wrangler sat at the front of the line of traffic.

Minutes later they were in the community of Winter Garden on a pleasant road that had two carriageways either side of a well-tended and attractive median.

Rick turned into a subdivision of similar two storey houses, many with pools. The development was set out in a circle with two more streets crossing the middle of the circle and intersecting at the centre of the circle.

As Rick turned right, Dom turned left to avoid the appearance of being on Rick's tail. By the time Dom had circumnavigated the estate and reached Rick's house, the equivalent of nine o clock on a clock face, the Wrangler was on the driveway and Rick was petting a golden retriever, which didn't seem exceptionally excited about the return of its master.

Dom didn't like dogs present at his crime scenes. They were unpredictable, and sometimes vicious. Luckily, this particular dog, her name was Winnie, looked to be neither, and so the serial killer relaxed a little.

Dom drove on past the Wrangler and parked fifty yards away by the side of the road. As he wrote down the address, he noted that the house number was in the five thousands, even though there were less than two hundred houses on the estate, he imagined such erratic numbering was a Southern thing. He also wondered what lay behind the decision to call the estate Winter Hills when there was no more than fifty feet of change in elevation across the whole county.

As he wrote in his Moleskine notebook, the door of the house opened, and Rick hugged a pretty young woman on the doorstep. She had long dark hair and had the look of her mother, Nikki from the YouTube videos.

First a dog and now a potential third person in the house. This was getting trickier by the minute, but Dom knew that he could not wait long. The video could be shared anytime, and he would be exposed.

He would return tomorrow evening, when the couple usually pre-recorded a weekly catch up to be released on a Friday. He intended to be ready for anything. He would bring his handgun.

Don't Miss the Tragic, Don't Miss the Gun!

Nikki was chatting with Jennie, the graphic designer for the Rix Flix brand on her cell phone.

"We've been given some great pictures that we'd like you to incorporate in the next video intro. We can send them by email. Hold on, I'm putting you on speaker. You can listen to the intro while it's still fresh in Rick's mind. Then we'll chat some more about a new segment we might try."

Nikki set the phone down flat on the desk, out of sight of the cameras, and posed with Rick. Side by side they faced the camera. Background looked OK; lighting looked fine. Door closed, no distracting noises. They were ready to go.

The bright video lights made the computer screens hard to see but they had done this many times. They knew when they were in shot and when they were not. The inability to read off screen was one of the reasons that they printed out the questions sent in by subscribers.

With the camera set high and above the laptop and desktop computers, the effect was flattering. Many people commented on how healthy and attractive the couple looked, but Nikki suspected that the camera might have an in-built filter. Rick had no such thoughts; he knew very well that it was simply because he was a handsome guy.

Rick was halfway through the intro when the door handle turned. He stopped speaking, cursing at first because it had been a word-perfect first take until then.

A moment later he recalled that they were supposed to be alone in the house and so there should be no-one around to turn the handle.

***

Dom had parked his rusty Bronco around the corner, out of sight of Rick and Nikki's grey painted two storey. The street was quiet. There was no-one around and the darkness engulfed him as he walked along the street dressed in black with his hood up and a medical mask covering his nose and mouth.

He walked around house to the rear where the Lanai stretched the entire length of the dwelling and covered the swimming pool and a generous patio. He looked up. The den lights were on. They were very bright; video lights, he guessed. This was a good result.

With his hunting knife he cut a hole in the plastic mesh cover of the lanai door, reached inside, and unlatched the door from the inside. He didn't worry about leaving fingerprints as he was wearing blue surgical gloves, the skin-tight latex shielding his identity.

The far door, a single door, was protected by a pool access alarm, as was the sliding patio door, as required by State law. Dom turned the knob. It moved easily. It was not locked from the inside. It was probably used to let the dog in and out all day and therefore would only be locked at night.

He pressed the outside button silencing the alarm. He had fifteen seconds to enter, close the door and press the internal button before the pool access alarm sounded loudly. He found the button and pressed it with seconds to go. Relief swept over him until he saw two eyes peering at him from the dog basket. The dog was illuminated from the lights in the kitchen.

The dog raised its head, the beginnings of a growl in its throat. It was puzzled. Dom moved over to the dog and scratched behind his ears. "Hey there, fella," he said quietly feeding the dog a tasty treat, "you just get some rest." As he scratched behind its ears the dog's eyes went dreamy and half closed. Petting was petting, the dog really didn't mind who was doing the petting.

Dom passed through the dimly lit lower floor, clearing it as he went. No-one was downstairs. With any luck only the two homeowners were in tonight.

He crept up the stairs which were thickly carpeted and silent under foot. Only one door showed a light beneath it. He checked the other rooms, just in case, but they were all empty. So far, so good. He had once been told that carpenters deliberately left space at the bottom of each door to allow the air conditioning to circulate. He wasn't sure it was true. It could have been an old carpenter's story to explain the poor fitting of a door.

Dom reached out and took hold of the door handle. He was about to turn it when he had a thought. What if, on the other side of the door, the couple were in the throes of passion? He then reasoned that there was little chance of that happening. This was a couple who had been married for over twenty years. When you got to a certain age you scheduled these things for the weekend, Friday night at best. No, he would be fine on a Thursday night. After all, they had work tomorrow.

***

Jennie enjoyed her part time role as a graphic designer for RixFlix and their road trips. She had also provided artwork for *PerpSearch*. She had been discussing some new ideas with Nikki when Rick declared that he was ready for a first take and it was always wise to allow Rick to record while the ideas were still in his head. He had retired from the corporate world, and with it most forms of planning and writing, some time ago.

So, Jennie sat quietly listening to Rick's opening sequence as it was recorded for the cameras many miles away. As she shuffled some papers on her desk Jennie noticed that Rick had stopped talking part way through the introduction. Thinking that the call had dropped she picked up the phone, only to discover that the call was still in progress.

What she heard next chilled her to the very core.

***

Dom's plan was simple - retrieve the video, wipe the various hard drives in the house, then do the same for the phones. Once the two vloggers had met his demands he would leave. The two vloggers, unfortunately, would never leave their house again on their own two feet. Still, they could still be famous as victims six and seven of the Symbol Slayer. He reached into his pocket and retrieved two wooden cubes crudely carved with Chinese symbols. Happy that he would have conveyed his misleading message to the authorities, he allowed the cubes to drop back into his pocket.

In less than twenty-four hours Dom would be on a flight to Manchester, England, on a tourist charter plane from Sanford. When he arrived, he would take the train to London and to the apartment his employers believed he had been occupying for the last few weeks.

When he arrived at the apartment, he would call California and explain that he was ready to return to work. Dominic would cease to be and an immaculately groomed Carswell would return to the USA with a rock solid alibi.

***

The door handle turned, and the door opened. Rick was about to rise and face the intruder when he was invited to sit back down by the waving of a large handgun. He complied.

Nikki was more frightened than she had ever been, except for when she was obliged to ride the Slingshot. That was still scarier.

"Who are you? What do you want?" Rick asked the intruder, who was dressed in black from head to foot. Even his Covid facemask was black. All that could be seen of the man under his hood was a wisp of blond hair and two intense blue eyes. There was cruelty behind those eyes and in an instant Rick and Nikki knew that they were facing a serial killer.

He seemed to be smiling behind the mask. His voice was educated, calm and authoritative. "I needed to speak to you."

Nikki responded, as much for the open telephone line to Jennie as to the killer.

"We have email addresses and phones, there's no need to invade our house brandishing a handgun." The man stepped around the desk and, grabbing a handful of cables, yanked them all out of their sockets.

The video lights went off, the computer monitor went dark and the diode on the microphone disappeared. He pushed down the lid of the laptop and stood back, admiring his handiwork. He had no intention of making an unexpected appearance on YouTube.

Once he was happy that they were not being recorded he issued his first instruction. "I want the original of the video you intend to broadcast on PerpSearch and all digital copies. Later, together, we will wipe it from any server where it may be stored. I know you will comply because I know you want to live."

Rick took the USB containing the video footage from the desk tidy and handed it over.

"I don't know why you are so desperate to have the video. It shows nothing of interest, as the police would happily tell you."

The intruder pocketed the USB stick and replied, "There must be something on it of interest or you wouldn't be showing it next week. So, tell me, what does it show? And don't spare me any details. Remember I will be checking, and if I find you are lying, I will return, with a less friendly demeanour."

"This is a friendly demeanour?" Rick asked himself silently before Nikki chipped in.

"The video was given to us by an old lady who had two valuable statues at the gate of her property. The statues were stolen and recovered; she didn't want them to go missing again."

Recognition flashed in Dom's eyes, and he laughed. "Are we talking about the two gargoyles?"

"Yes. They're valuable, they're cast from the same moulds as the originals that once sat either side of the Universal Studios entrance," Nikki explained.

Dom laughed out loud. "No one in their right mind would steal those. Anyway, continue." He pointed at Nikki with the gun and so she continued.

"One camera faces the road and caught four vehicles heading towards the camera. Three local vehicles and a Silver Grey Bronco. The police have already ruled out the local vehicles."

"Could you identify the driver through the windscreen?" Dom asked. He knew if that was the case, the police might be able to trace him through facial recognition. He didn't wear a mask in the car.

"No. The reflections on the windscreen made it impossible."

"You said there was a second camera."

"The second camera was concealed in a bush. It was intended to capture the features of any thief." Nikki paused. "All it showed was the back of the Bronco from the truck bed up. It showed a Seminoles graphic on the rear windscreen."

"Well, as you seem to be quite the detective, what were you able to discern from this 'useless' footage that was worth showing on YouTube?"

"Our graphic designer couldn't get a face from the front shot, but she was able to blow up a sticker on the front windscreen. It was too pixelated to read but Google Eye and image search software showed an FSU parking sticker. It was orange and the University confirmed that the orange stickers were issued in 2017. In 2022 the stickers are purple. So, we speculated that the killer might be a former FSU student who supported the Seminoles."

***

Jennie called 911 on her landline, keeping the cell phone line open. Despite living hundreds of miles from Winter Garden, she was speaking to the Orange County Sherriff's despatcher within a minute.

She had explained the situation to a very sceptical deputy before being re-routed back to the despatcher. The despatcher was a calm lady whose voice was light and controlled.

"We have two mobile units in the immediate vicinity. They will be at the house in two minutes. The Orlando Police HRT, armed Hostage Rescue Team, will take fifteen minutes to get to the location but hopefully our deputies can manage the situation until then."

Jennie was not convinced.

***

Nikki was good. The young man who had sold the car to Dom for cash had been an FSU student, but the Seminoles graphic was a relic of the car's early history further up north in Florida. Carswell could use a woman like Nikki in his next campaign, but that just wasn't possible.

"How come you have managed to kill five girls and only two are being followed up? Where are the others?"

Aware that in the movies he would now explain the whole plot just before he killed the curious victim, he hesitated. In movies the victim often survived, only to send the killer to the death row. However, he had the gun in his hand. What was the harm?

"Covid 19 had a big part to play. I travelled across six states to get here. The other three girls are in Arizona, Texas and Alabama. To be honest, I hoped that the Chinese carvings would link all of the cases, but it appears not. Although all murders are now routinely logged with the Department of Justice, for exactly this reason - to track killers across states - the database is way out of date. Illness, death, working from home and pandemic isolation has decimated the admin staff used to update the database. They're still inputting data for 2020."

Dominic reached into his pocket and retrieved two polished wooden blocks. They were cubes, measuring approximately an inch and a half in each direction. On one side of each block was a carved Chinese symbol. He dropped them on the desk. Rick and Nikki picked up one each.

Neither of the vloggers understood Chinese, but they both knew instinctively that the blocks contained the Chinese characters for the numbers six and seven.

A Sticky Situation

Dominic thought he saw a hint of blue and then red light shining through the window around the drawn venetian blind. He stepped forward and pulled up a single slat to look outside.

Two Sherriff's vehicles were moving speedily down the road immediately outside the sub-division. They turned off their lights and sirens as he watched. Theirs was to be a stealth approach, rookie error keeping the blues and reds on a minute too long. Dom swore.

"You called the police, somehow you called the police!" He was not shouting, he was not complaining, he was stating a fact. He could have looked for the silent alarm or whatever it was they had pressed, but it was irrelevant now.

"Until a few minutes ago you had not seen my face, you knew nothing about me. Given time you would have cleared all your hard drives for me and there wouldn't have been a problem. Now? Well, now, we have a hostage situation."

Rick and Nikki knew he was lying. They knew they were destined to die in this small den, amidst their memorabilia and memories. Why else would the little blocks with the Chinese symbols be sitting on the desk?

"Look," Rick said in his most persuasive voice (you learn a lot when you have had a career in sales). "You're going to be apprehended anyway, so why hurt us? It's pointless, and It'll obviously increase your sentence." He paused and looked at Nikki, who was obviously just as scared as he was. "We could speak on your behalf. We could tell the Judge that you had a chance to harm us, but you showed compassion, kindness even. It must help."

Dom removed his mask and smiled. His was a kind face, It was not the face of a serial killer. "You can't kid a kidder, Rick." His voice and demeanour changed in an instant, even the way he stood and held himself changed. It was like looking at a different person. The two hostages were puzzled.

"I am brainstorming here, so give me a little leeway. I am thinking that if I kill you both, shoot myself in the arm and then put the gun in your dead hand, I can argue the gun was yours and you shot first. In the struggle that followed I managed to overpower you and shoot you, but sadly Nikki got caught in the crossfire."

"No-one is going to believe that, it's ridiculous!" Rick blurted, whilst wondering if a jury might just believe this smooth-talking man.

"Is it? I can be very persuasive. I have been ill recently, and I am on heavy medication. Maybe I forgot to take my meds and can't remember why I was here. I am thinking that if one juror sees things my way, maybe I avoid a felony murder charge.

OK. I serve a few short years for unlawful killing. But I can live with that. I have friends who would make sure I was in a comfortable Federal Facility."

"That's insane," Nikki interjected. "You killed five women."

"Did I, though? They haven't been able to prove anything yet, and without you two around they will not necessarily link any of those deaths with yours."

"We have the death penalty here. Let us go and we'll speak at any clemency hearing." Rick was grasping at straws; the man was unbalanced.

"I won't be tried in Florida. My lawyer will ask for me to be tried in California where the first murder happened. The other deaths will be taken into consideration in that trial. I have the kind of friends who can make that happen." Dominic smiled mirthlessly at the two of them. "Sorry, Nikki I kind of like you, but then I liked them all – just before the end."

His expression changed and he adopted a thousand-yard stare. Something was going on in his twisted mind that they did not care to know.

***

Nikki could not contain the tears. They escaped her eyes and trickled down her cheeks. Their children, their parents their friends, all would suffer and mourn. The madman before them had no reason to keep them alive. As she reached forward to take a tissue, her knee brushed against something under the desk. There was something leaning against the pedestal that should not be there. She sneaked a look and saw what was within her grasp.

Dominic looked away when he saw the tears. He glanced out of the window. The Sheriff's deputies were standing by their cars, positioning themselves for action. Each was holding a long gun. They were loaded for bear, as the saying goes.

He stood still, his hand resting by his side, the gun pointing at the floor temporarily. He sighed heavily. He'd had plans, ambitions. He had planned a glorious future for himself, but it was never going to happen now. He put the mask back on.

Nikki leaned forward in her seat, dabbing her eyes with a tissue in her left hand whilst wrapping her had around the object under the table. Her fingers blindly found their place, and she was ready.

***

Dom was surprised when Nikki pushed back her chair quickly. He was about to raise his gun and fire when he saw her jump to her feet and aim a plastic Nerf type gun at him. He laughed and dropped his hand back to his side. Her toy weapon was colourful, in shades of bright red and blue, with an oversized barrel, but it was still a toy. It was no more deadly than a water pistol.

"Are you going to shoot me, Nikki?" he mocked.

Nikki aimed at the man's hand, the one holding the gun, and pulled the trigger on the Web Slinger.

The CO^2 did its job and sent the web hurtling along the barrel, the two-part resin sprayed just as it was supposed to, and the sticky web opened up on ejection. In a second the web hit its target and wrapped itself around the hand, the gun and the man's leg.

Dom laughed at first when the spider web landed. He was about to break into a rendition of the TV Spiderman theme song, in mockery of the failed attempt to disable him, when he felt a stinging pain in his hand.

Wherever the joint of the web connected with his hand it hurt. It was burning. He tried to lift up his hand to pull off the offending web, but it was stuck to his trouser leg, and the gun with it. His hand was bright red, and the former burning sensation was now a certifiable pain. The more he pulled, the tighter it got. He tried to pull it off with his left hand, but the web had dried in seconds and the threads between the veins of the web were immovable.

"Damn you!" he yelled. "You die first!" He pulled off the mask with his left hand. He needed to breathe; he was beginning to panic.

At that very moment the Web Slinger hissed a second time, and another web flew towards its target. This time Nikki was aiming at Carswell's face, and she found her target.

The web attached itself to the man's face when his mask was half on and half off. He had blinked automatically when he heard the hiss and one eye was glued shut, one half open. His lips were stuck together on the right side of his face, leaving his face twisted and deformed.

He yelled an obscenity from the open part of his mouth and made a determined effort to release the gun.

There was a loud bang, a mist of red blood spatter, and Nikki fell to the floor.

***

The two deputies had been instructed to wait for the Orlando Police but when they heard the shot they reacted and kicked in the front door. The time for waiting had gone. They racked their guns and prepared to fire.

***

Rick dived on top of Nikki in an effort to protect her, but he knew he was too late. As he landed, he spoke gently into her ear as she lay face down.

"Nikki, if you live through this, I won't just paint that wall, I'll paint the whole damn house." He realised that he was crying. This was not just the love of his life, this was his life.

"Is that a promise?" Nikki asked in a normal, steady voice, not one racked with pain or frozen in panic.

"You were shot," Rick said incredulously, as he rose and checked Nikki for signs of injury. There were none. "I saw the blood."

"Not mine. I think our mad friend shot himself in the foot."

Indeed, he had. In his manic attempts to free the gun, he had pulled the trigger and shot a large hole in his foot.

Rick jumped to his feet and ran around the desk to ensure that their would-be assailant was neutralised. The man was yelling in agony and panic. He tried to bend down to hold his damaged foot, hoping the pressure would ease the pain. As he began to fold his body, Rick stood behind him and, out of sight of his wife, put his meaty hand on the back of the man's head, slamming it into the desktop.

The moaning stopped. Carswell collapsed to the floor, unconscious.

"What happened?" Nikki asked as she rose from her position behind the desk.

"I think he passed out from the pain and banged his head on the desk on the way down." Nikki didn't believe him, but she didn't care either way. This awful man would kill no more.

"Armed police, kneel on the floor, hands interlocked on your head, or we shoot on entry!" The door burst open, and two deputies stormed in, shotguns levelled.

Rick and Nikki had their hands on their heads. "I think we have the situation under control," Rick said, smiling.

Epilogue

Orlando Sentinel

Metro Section – Staff Reporter

California Governor Hopeful found Guilty

> After two days of Jury considerations and a further day for psychological reports, Judge Robert T Handsford, handed down the judgement in the Carswell Judd trial.
> Judd was found guilty of five counts of first-degree murder, kidnap, false imprisonment, assault with a deadly weapon and fifteen lesser charges.
> He will serve five consecutive life sentences, meaning that he has no hope of parole.

***

Rick read the online press article out aloud, as Nikki listened. The man would die in prison, that was justice, but it could never replace those precious lives, those lost opportunities, those lost futures, those lost children.

Six months had now passed since they had posted *Zero Days Without Incident*, six months since the most terrifying night of their lives, and, six months since Nikki gave Rick a lecture about always keeping the lounge tidy, the pillows plumped and in their proper place on the couch and chairs.

She was right of course; you never knew when the Exterminator or Orlando SWAT were going to turn up and find the place generally untidy.

PerpSearch was now being run by Danielle Stankowski, Professor of Criminal Behaviour at FSU, and she was welcome to it.

The RixFlix and Roadtrips YouTube channels were going well, subscribers were up, and Jennie's new graphics were in demand on tee shirts and sweatshirts on the website

Today Rick had donned a yellow tee shirt, baseball cap and shoes. Nikki was at his side wearing a Hogwarts tee shirt, today was a big day at Universal Studios. The Revenge of the Mummy was re-opening, and they were going to ride it.

Original Cover Art

J JACKSON BENTLEY

THE HOOGFLPAFF ENIGMA

A Second RixFlix Short Story

Copyright J Jackson Bentley 2022

Edited by Susan Whitfield, Vice President, RixFlix

Published by Fidus USA
An imprint of www.FidusPress.com

All rights reserved. This is a work of fiction. Real world places, characters, and companies are re-imagined and used in a fictitious setting throughout. No similarity to actual real-life characteristics, actions or behaviours is intended. Where copyrighted and trademarked names, products or characters are mentioned, the ownership of those Intellectual Properties resides with their owners or licensees.

The cooperation and permissions of Rix Flix and its named owners, subscribers and followers is appreciated and applauded by the author. All proceeds to Rix Flix and Road trips Channels.

When the inspiration for the Hufflepuff Badger goes missing at an exhibition

Things begin to get out of hand for our intrepid duo.

Excerpt from JK Rowling Wikipedia Entry.

"Born in Yate, Gloucestershire, Rowling was working as a researcher and bilingual secretary for Amnesty International in 1990 when she conceived the idea for the Harry Potter series while on a delayed train from Manchester to London."

Edward the Elder Historical Official Biography

"Edward the Elder[a] (c. 874 – 17 July 924) was King of the Anglo-Saxons from 899 until his death in 924. He was the elder son of Alfred the Great and his wife Ealhswith. Edward inherited the title King of the Anglo Saxons when Alfred died in 899. He married Ecgwynn who bore him two children".

NB: It was also rumoured that he took a Danish Mistress, Helga, to appease the Danes who were previously opposed to his reign.

Introduction 1

Crewe Railway Station, England, Early 1990's.

The smartly dressed businesswoman was both annoyed and worried as she stood on the cold windswept London bound platform at Crewe Station. Her Manchester to London train had been scheduled to stop at this station, often described as the railway crossroads of England, but it was not expected to end its journey here. Her modern electric train limped into the sidings once its passengers had all disembarked onto a previously empty and uninviting platform.

The next stopping train to Kings Cross was not due for over ninety minutes. She and her fellow passengers were down on their luck as both the cafeteria and the waiting room were closed. The cafeteria closed promptly at 6pm and the waiting room was being refurbished, allegedly. How do you refurbish a big old modern Victorian waiting room with modern plastic chairs? You can't change the wall tiles or floor tiles as they are protected by the legislation for historic buildings. Likewise, the old fireplace that had not seen a fire since the second world war was sure to be listed. She supposed you could change the modern electric strip lighting, but how long should that take?

Resigned to her fate and unfamiliar with Crewe, with no money to spare, she left the station and looked for somewhere warm to sit for an hour or so.

After a few minutes walking the empty streets, her eyes alighted on the Crewe Museum and Historical Centre. It was well lit, welcoming, free of charge and it was open late. The old local museum shone like a beacon in the evening gloom that was so familiar to those travellers out and about in the British Mid-Winter.

She went inside and an elderly volunteer was soon at her side. The old lady took her by the arm and led her to a seat by the old column radiator.

"You look frozen, love," she said kindly." I have some tea on the brew. We'll both have a cuppa and then you can look around."

Warmed as much by her friendly welcome as by the tea, the younger woman browsed the exhibits. She passed displays for the War Years and the Industrial Revolution; they did not interest her. Then she saw the exhibit covering the Dark Ages and stood looking on in awe at an artefact that looked new, but which was actually a thousand years old.

She asked the old lady about the artefact.

"It should really be displayed in London, but the British Museum said they had far more artefacts than they could display already, and so here it is, on long term loan from the Earl of Deane." She opened the cabinet and allowed Joanne to hold the ancient relic. "It's a crudely formed badger. The white decoration is polished Marcasite, a crystal from of iron sulphide, and the rest is aged bronze."

"It looks like it's wearing a scarf," the businesswoman said, being somewhat fanciful. It took a good imagination to even see it was a badger, let alone identify its apparel.

"It was a gift to the mistress of Edward the Elder, second King of the Anglo-Saxons. It is said to be from around 900 AD."

Enchanted by the crude sculpture that was around six inches in length, she asked the elderly lady with genuine interest. "What was the mistress's name?"

"Her name was Helga Hoogflpaff. Many local people thought she was a witch."

The younger woman laughed. "Sounds a bit like Hoofflepuff, the way you say it." The old lady joined in the laughter and then the younger woman had an idea, a quite brilliant idea.

Introduction 2

Tempest High School, Central Florida, Early 1990's.

Across the Atlantic Ocean, in Florida, Nikki was trying out for the flag squad on the baseball field behind the high school. The Tempest Twirl & Flag squad enjoyed a stellar reputation in local competition, and so they didn't let just anyone into the squad; places had to be earned.

Nikki, with her good looks, trim figure and long flowing hair, had every chance of making the team, but only if she could manipulate the heavy flag during an arduous and quite complex routine.

After the first session everyone chilled out on the bleachers, hydrating with water, soda, and juice. The roar of a motorcycle engine alerted them to the arrival of a biker on the side road behind the baseball field. The motorcycle stopped and cut its engine. The tall, rangy rider took off his helmet to reveal the statutory long hair underneath.

"It's Rick," Marti announced. "My brother." The girls ran, as one, towards the older boy - with the exception of one single girl who showed no interest - Nikki.

Rick was a few years older than the high school girls but that didn't matter to his sister who seemed determined to play matchmaker for her 'lonely' older brother. Rick would have eschewed the word 'lonely' and replaced it with 'carefree'.

Nikki's impression was that the boy was showing off and she didn't need another self-centred man in her circle just now.

But sometimes things are just meant to be, and despite this tepid, if not chilly, introduction to Rick from a distance, fate would step in.

***

Nikki was a delightful young woman who charmed the adults she knew, and won friends by being constantly bright and cheerful, but sometimes bright and cheerful was just unachievable, like today.

She was heartbroken, distressed and a little disillusioned with men in general. Nikki and her long-term boyfriend had broken up. Like all teenagers in love, the world was over, it was a tragedy of Shakespearean proportions. She was Juliet, Ophelia and Cordelia rolled into one.

Nikki's dad was always able to lift her spirits at times of trouble, but even his urgent, and often comic, efforts drew little response. The flame was dimmed and getting dimmer by the day. Concerned for Nikki and her 'lonely' brother Rick, Marti contrived to set them up on a blind date.

Some days later, over a pizza followed by a scary movie, *The People Under the Stairs*, Rick and Nikki bonded. She was less convinced of the connection between them at first, but Rick felt the electricity immediately. He knew that he would pursue this girl until he won her heart, or she took out a restraining order against him.

***

Now, anyone who has been the father of a teenage girl knows that the last thing you want for your daughter is a hormonally driven, younger version of yourself, dating her.

Nikki's dad was no different. Rick had long hair and liked rock music – this produced, in his mind, the potential for a non-conformist hippy lifestyle for his grandkids. Rick was older than Nikki and therefore a threat to her virtue. Her dad dismissed that thought before it took hold in his imagination. Finally, and perhaps most worrying, Rick lacked direction. He should have earned his degree by now and had a career, but he had neither.

Still, romance finds a way, and Nikki was now as addicted to Rick as he was to her. The precious hours, minutes and seconds they spent together would barely compensate for the seemingly interminable, endless hours apart.

So, Rick went back to university as an older student, with fresh faced freshman Nikki attending the same school, and by the time they graduated they were a married couple in all but name.

Rick proposed and Nikki cried. And Rick has been making her cry ever since, with happiness of course.

LOYALTY 1

Diagon Alley, Universal Studios, Orlando 2022.

Defying the passing years since they married, an ever-youthful Nikki was riding piggy-back on Rick's larger frame. They had just apparated from Hogsmeade, with the aid of some Jennie video magic. The husband-and-wife vlogging team were visiting today, courtesy of Universal Orlando Media Team, to see the unveiling of a temporary exhibit in the auditorium that had once hosted the Fear Factor attraction. Rick and Nikki both had fond memories of sitting on the infamously uncomfortable aluminium bleacher benches, watching Bill and Ted's Halloween Adventures, as well as the Fear Factor itself.

Today, however, there was to be a presentation relating to the Wizarding World of Harry Potter, and RixFlix had been invited. Better still, Rick and Nikki were to be seated in the front row.

After standing in line, showing their various permits, and then standing in line again, they were allowed to file in. They had the best seats in the house, on the aisle at the front. A giant curtained backdrop covered the old film set that had hosted a Wild West Stunt Show decades before. The backdrop was black with tiny sparkling stars and was decorated with artwork relating to the film franchise. The Elder Wand, the Sign of the Deathly Hallows and various broomsticks were represented by golden line art.

In the centre of the backdrop was a large video screen carrying the promise of 'A Glimpse into The World of Wizards, Witches and Magic'. The writing was displayed in the ubiquitous Harry Potter font.

After the opening introduction by a beige suited cast member, the screen showed a short documentary about the artefacts, real and invented, used in the film series. For a limited period, the props and artefacts would be displayed in the Tribute Store beside the Mummy Ride.

When the now grown-up stars of the Warner Brothers films closed the video presentation with their wands pointing at the camera and saying in unison, "Ascendio", the large cloth covering the exhibits lifted, apparently magically, to reveal the rare and revered pieces.

The crowd clapped loudly and cheered enthusiastically, and Peter, the bespectacled Potter Collector, was on his feet urging the crowd on. Rick and Nikki, who were seated beside him, rose to their feet too. This was one magical collection, and one magical moment.

***

Peter Kenneth, known to his followers as the Potter Collector, ended the call to his mother. Theirs was a close relationship. He enjoyed telling her tales of his travels and she genuinely enjoyed hearing of them.

Catching up with Rick and Nikki, he asked, "What was your favourite item?" They looked at him as though the question was superfluous. Clearly the one-thousand-year-old badger was the most enthralling item in the collection. To add to the rarity of the piece, it was rumoured that it had once been a gift to Queen Consort Helga Hoogflpaff, the clear inspiration for Helga Hufflepuff, the founder of Rick's chosen Hogwarts house.

They walked briskly to the newly redecorated Tribute Store, now adorned with Wizarding World banners and symbols. A taped cordon snaked around beside the store between the store and the outcropping Rip Ride Rocket, in front of the New York skyline. Every person in the line was wearing something related to the Harry Potter universe. Some wore robes, but others were obvious cosplayers whose costumes were of varying quality. The most convincing personality in the line was Herbert Tolworth from Iowa, whose hair and beard were real, and whose appearance closely recalled the Richard Harris depiction of Albus Dumbledore.

Peter introduced himself to Dumbledore, unnecessarily as it turned out, and asked for a picture to be taken with the eccentric older gentleman. Herb agreed. He was a keen follower of Peter and often tuned in to watch the Potter Collector unboxing his new collectibles.

***

In less than an hour the artefacts would be safely back in their cabinets, where they had been for the last week, as Universal soft opened the store to staff and cast members, to huge acclaim.

Then the line would snake slowly forward, and the media invitees would get to see the props and artefacts up close. The centrepiece of the exhibition being the ancient Badger, in a security-controlled, tempered glass cocoon it was brightly spot lit. It was magical, it was breath-taking, it was real.

Rick and Nikki filed in through the Tribute Store entrance façade, carefully themed as it always was, to the exhibits inside. The space was lit with black light and neon. It was generally quite dark, not Halloween Horror Night House dark, but almost.

As they rounded the corner into the central core, they saw the Badger exhibit. It seemed to be lit by a light from heaven. There in the gloom stood a large crystalline pyramid cone covering the black badger with its white marcasite jewelling sparkling and bouncing rainbow shafts of light around the room.

Rick took in a deep breath and forgot to breathe out. Nikki's hand flew to her mouth and her eyes teared up. It was that impressive, it was that emotional.

An unwanted voice interrupted the moment, and everyone in the room was brought abruptly back to the present.

"The dome, actually more of a pyramid, is constructed from a specially formulated crystal glass toughened with plastics. It rests on a pressure sensor. Anyone attempting to the lift the glass will set off an alarm that will lock the Tribute Store doors, all of the safety lights will be illuminated and the Hoogflpaff Badger will be moved to a safe place whilst we investigate. Cutting a hole in the glass would also set off the sensitive alarm, and so we think our treasure is safe. And we want to share it with you."

If they had been impressed before, the crowd were now dumbfounded. As soon as the announcer stopped talking, green lasers ran all over the badger as if scanning it and then, in the darkness above the exhibit, a large three-dimensional outline version of the badger appeared. Once the lasers had light painted the wireframe of the static badger in the darkness, it suddenly became animated. It turned its head, looked at the crowd and, apparently startled, it turned and ran off, its scarf flapping around its neck.

This time there was a group intake of breath, manic clapping, unrestrained cheering and shouts of 'Go, Badger, Go!'

One older lady, perhaps inappropriately dressed as Hermione, fainted.

Peter, the Potter Collector, filmed the whole process through misted eyes.

LOYALTY 2

Evesham, United Kingdom, 2022.

Andy Giles looked forlornly out of the window. The English weather had been particularly foul today. It had peppered his office window with all of the weapons it had at its disposal - rain, wind, sleet. Dark clouds mottled the sky, not quite recreating the Dark Mark, but with a good imagination, you could make out the outline of a skull. He was now back at home, but the weather had not improved. As a Detective Sergeant he probably should still have been at his desk, but he had already logged enough hours this week to fill a month of timesheets.

Heavy rain was tapping out a staccato drumbeat on the window glass and the wind howled. The stiff breeze forced its way through the jambs of the elderly double glazing, finding any tiny crevice it could exploit to create a continuous tuneless whistle. Andy was feeling miserable. His partner entered the room unseen behind him and, sensing Andy's mood from his slumped shoulders, said: "Not to worry, it's almost time to get your fix!"

This innocent fix was unrelated to drug abuse or even alcohol. The fix in question was sunny Florida, the fix was, more precisely, RixFlix. It was 5:45pm in the UK but in Florida it was approaching 1pm and Rick's live stream from Universal Studios was beckoning.

A couple of hours sitting in front of his large screen TV watching the big, yellow clad Vlogster wandering around the theme park in the sunshine was just what was required.

Andy logged in and found that the YouTube timer was ticking away.

"Pinocchio: Hey Andy how's things?"

"Ready for another livestream mate." Andy responded, feeling uplifted already. Here was a community, a family that he had never met and probably never would meet, some cynics might say the best kind of family. Andy relaxed on his armchair with the keyboard on his lap and a

cup of strong builders' tea at his side. The wine could wait until after his evening meal. Eating would wait until Rick was winding down for the day and thinking of his own lunch.

Andy sighed. How he wished that he, too, could be in Florida, aimlessly wandering around the theme park, obviously not fully appreciating the great care and detailed planning[1] that Rick put into these midweek trips.

***

Rick set the camera down so that it was overlooking Louie's Bar & Grill and the bridge carrying the Hogwarts Express. He was sipping from a cup of water when a man in a dark blue suit and tie approached him.

"Rick, of Rix Flix fame I'm guessing," the man said, extending his hand.

"What gave me away?" Rick joked as he shook the outstretched hand. The man looked puzzled, shook his head, and continued. Not an individual with a great sense of humour, Rick was guessing.

"Yes, quite." The voice was English, and the man was using received pronunciation, that standard form of British English pronunciation, based on educated speech in southern England, widely accepted as the real British accent elsewhere in the world. "When you have finished filming, perhaps you could come and see me at the Tribute Store. Ask for "Mr Barrington," he said, pointing at his name badge. The company name on the badge was SportsSec and Rick was intrigued.

***

Ginger Princess set down her glass. Another fabulous virtual trip to Orlando via YouTube had ended.

"Bye everyone!" she typed as she sighed.

---

[1] Rick, detailed planning. Ha, Ha, Ha. JJB is letting his imagination run wild here. Nikki.

She would have liked a little more filming in Diagon Alley. She loved the place, she felt at home there when she visited. Perhaps it was her hair colour. A lifetime redhead, actually a genuine ginger, she had always considered herself to be one of the Weasley clan's distant American cousins.

She had a few minutes before she had to head out and so picked up her favourite magazine, Ellery Queen. She loved a mystery.

***

Several states away *Alisha, of Books and Things*, turned off her laptop, which was sitting on the bookshop counter and turned to serve a customer. 'I wonder who the man in the suit was in the livestream?' she thought as she placed a copy of 'Nancy Drew and the Deviant Diva' into an eco-friendly brown bag with a string handle.

***

Rick exited the park and filmed his 'extro', telling everyone not to miss the magic or the fun. He closed off the livestream before his phone died altogether and then retraced his steps back into the park for his mysterious meeting.

Miss America scanned him in and joined in with his banter, then he walked down towards the now defunct Shrek ride, past the big yellow New York taxi, that he had nicknamed Maxi, waving to Labby the Cabby as he went.

Two minutes later he stood outside the Tribute Store, bedecked as it was with a banner proclaiming its term as the home of the *Harry Potter Exhibition of Arte-Facts & Fun!*

Inside the store was a distraught looking woman in a universal uniform. She blew her nose and dabbed at her tearful eyes as she directed Rick inside to where Mr Barrington was waiting.

***

Rick signed a piece of paper that declared itself to be an NDA, a non-disclosure agreement, before he was allowed to be told about the disaster that had unfolded in the Tribute Store the day before. The press could not hear about it, nor could the foundation that funded the exhibits. Secrecy was demanded.

When he signed the sheet headed with the SportSec logo he asked if he could now officially be regarded as a secret agent, a spy of sorts! The man frowned and said no, bluntly. Rick took that as a yes and made a note to have the website changed to reflect his new status.

"Rick, the Hoogflpaff Badger has been stolen. We don't know how, security here is as tight as it was for the Hope Diamond, but it has vanished into thin air."

Rick was no follower of the arts and had not been in a museum since, well, he would have to check with his mum – that's how long ago it was. Nonetheless, even he knew the Hope Diamond was worth $300 million.

"So, Rick, we need you and Nikki to help us solve the mystery of its disappearance and help us get it back."

Rick laughed.

"This is a matter for the police, surely."

"They are mystified, and they said that there was little chance of recovering such a small piece when it could have been taken by any one of hundreds of staff and tens of thousands of theme park visitors." He paused shaking his head. "The truth is, they are assigning a detective, but we do not believe that they will make much progress."

"But why me? I'm no detective."

"You and Nikki brought to justice a serial killer who had evaded the police in six states and the FBI. Who has a better resume?"

Rick should have argued that the killer actually found them, but he was busy mentally re-imaging the website, adding his new twin roles of secret agent and detective.

The man continued to his last argument. "Besides, you are a confirmed member of the Hufflepuff community, you wear their colours. Loyalty is their watchword! Are you going to fail them in their hour of need?"

Trapped with words. Damn it, Rick needed to be quicker on his feet. He would think of a smart answer this afternoon, for sure, but then it would be too late. The man had already invited himself to RixFlix Manor deep in the heart of Winter Garden to meet Nikki, the second detective in the mix.

On his way home Rick puzzled over how he had gone from a Rix Flix partnership with Nikki to becoming *Hart to Hart*, in three sentences. He puzzled over it until his puzzler was sore. 'Hart to Hart', he daydreamed briefly of Stephanie Powers at her best. The eighties were a great decade. But would Nikki be impressed with her new role? Unlikely, he thought.

PATIENCE

3209 Wintermere Grove, Winter Gardens, Florida

Rick and Nikki had moved house after what they called the 'Big Incident' at their old house. Their elderly dog, Winnie, didn't approve of the move but was placated with a comfortable new bed and a constant supply of Blue Buffalo dog treats. She had been, quite literally, in the doghouse after welcoming in a serial killer in return for a few dog biscuits, but now all was forgiven.

The new house was in a recent development called Wintermere Gardens, not too far from the Village Mall, where you could buy almost anything.

The house was what Nikki described as her dream house. It was two storey, four bedroomed with an In-Law Suite. There was also a separate diner, which was now a video studio. The patio doors led out to the deck, pool, and hot tub. "It's hard work walking around theme parks all day" was Rick's winning argument, so for the sake of an extra $10 a month on the mortgage for a hot tub, Nikki was not prepared to make a stand.

The house walls were generally a sandy coloured stucco with slightly orangey architectural features around the windows and doors. It was OK outside, but it was the inside that sold Nikki. The light and airy house had space to spare and lots of storage. One complete closet was dedicated to living room pillows that could be changed out from season to season.

Another selling point was the In-Law suite which had its own bathroom, small kitchen, external door and, importantly, a lockable door into the main house. Privacy was paramount when you were as busy as Rick and Nikki.

So, Nicki's idea of an *Airbnb* apartment where followers could come and stay at their favourite vloggers' house, was soon to be a reality. They already had a tentative booking from the Landon family, who regularly joined in livestream chats under the screen name *TwistedSista*, which was a bit worrying to Nikki. The Landons explained the name was a joke based on an experience at HHN 25. Rick, ever optimistic, pointed out that the television actor Michael Landon had always been a really nice guy in series like Little House on the Prairie and Highway to Heaven, and this family shared the same surname.

After all of these wonderful years of marriage, and despite her inner voice warning to the contrary, Nikki was still inexplicably comforted by Rick's insane logic.

As for the rest of the house, much of the memorabilia that had been confined to a couple of rooms in the old house now adorned various rooms in the new house. The downstairs of their new home was exquisitely tiled, but the stairs and upper floor were fully carpeted.

Nikki was tidying up. After all, a visitor was expected. She sighed. Rick's Shrek 4D glasses and crudely 3D printed blue wax model of Jaws had found their way from the drawer, back onto her display shelves. She put them back in the drawer and hoped that Rick would forget about them for a while.

The landline phone rang. The security guard at the gate of the new community had just allowed in a Mr Barrington of SportSec, who was heading to their house.

***

"My name is Barrington, Terrence Barrington." The man in the dark suit had a Christian name, apparently.

Nikki, who had answered the door, was tempted to make the obvious allusion to 'My name is Bond, James Bond', but Mr Barrington did not look like a man who enjoyed jokes at his expense.

Barrington had vocally approved of the décor, describing it as militaristic in its attention to detail but comfortably feminine in its layout. Nikki basked for a moment in the warm glow that the compliment had augured. Then, over the next twenty minutes, he explained his problem, now their problem.

It turned out that SportSec were a worldwide security organisation who had begun life protecting sports venues but who now covered Theme Parks and other mass attendance venues. They had been approached to provide security to the travelling Harry Potter Exhibition and had done so meritoriously until now - Mr Barringtons's words.

Then a mystery had unfolded in front of their eyes, and they were at a loss to understand what they could have done better. He described the day of the theft.

"The Tribute Store had opened at 7am to allow cast members to browse through the exhibits before the park was opened to guests. It was quiet, in fact there were only six people in the Tribute Store when the theft occurred. They were," - he read from a list:

1) Estelle Stevens (Marilyn Monroe) already in costume.
2) Taylor McCort (Beetlejuice) in costume.
3) Gerald Hadley (Labby the Cabby) partly in costume.
4) Graham Pierce (Doc Brown) not in costume.
5) David Parkin, ride attendant.
6) Lucy Drake, merchandise manager.

It was 7:47am and the alarm sounded. The doors were locked and supervised whilst I checked things out. No-one was in the room where the badger had disappeared, and no-one would admit that they were in the room when the alarm sounded. I suspected it was another false alarm, we had them before, but when I arrived the badger was gone."

The man was distraught but was also genuinely puzzled.

"We searched the cast members, intimately, and allowed them to leave. Then we spent the whole day searching the building with detectors of every kind. There was no brass and marcasite badger in the store, and we searched everywhere, even in the rafters. It simply disappeared."

"Perhaps it was never there." Rick set his mind back to the 1970's TV series Banacek, which he had been binge watching on Peacock TV. The man had solved many impossible crimes, just like this one.

"Perhaps," Rick postulated, "It vanished overnight and only a projection was seen on the day of the theft. Turn off the projection and hey presto, Badger disappears." The theory has sounded fine in his head, but out loud it was not as convincing.

The faces of Nikki and Barrington told him all he needed to know about their opinions on his theory. Barrington spoke.

"Actually, the inside of the glass is cleaned every day by one of my men, Evan, and the artifact is dusted with a special feathered wand that attracts the dust to it fibres.

Evan was quite insistent that the badger was present when he cleaned the glass and dusted. Also, the six visitors confirmed that the exhibit had been in place when they saw it, seconds before it disappeared into the ether."

***

Once Barrington had left and Nikki had plumped the pillows, the married couple sat down at the table and talked. Nikki began.

"Rick, I really don't know if we can help. Hufflepuff loyalty aside, I don't think that the traditional Hufflepuff patience and hard work will be enough. We need someone who has experience of these things, perhaps one of our followers."

"JJB writes thrillers and crime novels, he may have some insights," Rick responded. Nikki nodded but she was looking for real life expertise.

"Maybe you could make a subtle comment about the theft on the livestream and see if anyone could help us out."

They both decided that was a great idea and could hardly wait for "Saturyaay" Night to come along.

***

Nikki tossed and turned in bed. Her sleep was punctuated with short but vivid dreams of badgers, thieves and mysterious figures in the shadows of the Tribute Store.

When she awoke, she had a bright idea. Rick was taking the car for a service and tyre rotation, so she took her own car and, armed with the vlogging camera and its dead cat covered microphone, she set off to Universal Studios.

HARD WORK 1

The Tribute Store, Universal Orlando, Florida

Nikki's request for a quiet room to interview the staff about the theft was met immediately. It seems that behind the Tribute Store and Macy's, and beside the Mummy ride, was a comfortable lounge. It was left over from when customers were waiting to shoot a scene at the JVC Star Trek Adventure in the 1990's. Since then, it had been variously used as a meeting room, storage room and, most recently, a Green Room for visiting guests and celebrities who were opening rides or making guest appearances.

The room was large, and the walls were green, for greenscreen purposes Nikki assumed, and was laid out with elderly but comfortable leather sofas and chairs.

Nikki sat on one of the big armchairs, her legs tucked under her like they often were as a teenager. It made her feel comfortable, at home. She had a computer tablet and a notebook and pen. The notebook was actually a Hogwarts School Exercise Book. In it she had made a note of the questions that had interrupted her night of sleep.

Ten minutes after ensconcing herself in the private room the door opened, and a handsome young man looked in. He smiled; it was a great smile.

"Hi Nikki, I'm Evan. Terrence has asked me to speak to you." Somehow Nikki had expected Evan to have a British accent, possibly even a Welsh accent, but he evidently originally hailed from New Jersey. Nikki spotted the much-subdued accent because she herself hailed from that same area.

Nikki invited Evan to make himself comfortable and explained that she wanted to cover every event from the badger's arrival several days before, until the theft.

Evan sat on the sofa facing Nikki. He tucked his right ankle behind his left knee, unconsciously mimicking Nikki's own comfortable position.

"Well," he began, "it has been a weird week for me. I'm not a particularly spiritual man but when I held the badger for the first time, I couldn't just feel its weight, its heft, if you like. But - and I know that this sounds fanciful - I could feel a power emanating from it, almost like electricity. The cold brass seemed to be warm, in fact in my mind I felt that it was showing its approval of being held by me." He laughed, embarrassed, and Nikki smiled. She had felt this same feeling several times during her life but mostly when she had a child in her arms, or she was brushing one of her girls' hair. Still, she knew what Evan meant, and she could imagine why the feeling would seem alien to a man dedicated to a prosaic job like security. Evan continued.

"Two days ago, the alarm sounded, again by the time I arrived there was no-one in the room. The last two people in the room had been Labby the Cabby and Miss America, as Rick calls her. Labby was pushing her wheelchair and helping her negotiate the tight corners in the dark rooms.

I looked into the cabinet and the badger was there, unmoved and safe. I lifted the glass cover and the alarm sounded again. I set the cover down squarely, so that it had maximum contact with the strip pressure pad around its perimeter. Finding all to be well, I began to leave the room. Then, I noticed something was missing.

The warm glow I felt in the presence of the badger had disappeared. Perhaps I had been imagining it all along, who knows."

Nikki made a note of Evan's feeling. When an artifact disappeared as if by magic, magic could well be the key to finding it again. Evan concluded.

"Much to their annoyance I frisked Labby and Miss America, but they were clean. Honestly, I don't know what I expected to find."

***

Nina Santiago was the next person to be interviewed. She had been assigned to the Tribute Store since the badger arrived. She sat more formally on the sofa and gave an account of everything that had happened on her watch. Where she had coincided with Evan, her story was identical to his.

Nikki was perplexed. Nothing she had heard gave any clue as to what could have happened to make the badger simply vanish from sight. There had to be an answer, but it escaped her, at least for the time being.

The next person to adorn the sofa, and she did it so well, was Estelle Stevens, otherwise known to park guests as Marilyn Monroe. Despite the fact that she was being formally interviewed, she remained in character. Her glamorous white gown was pristine and all consuming. She looked like every man's dream of what a Fifties woman would be. Nikki felt dowdy and underdressed in her presence.

Estelle explained that on the day of the theft she was accompanied by Graham Pierce (Doc Brown), and that Labby the Cabby and Beetlejuice had allowed her to go into the store first, leaving her a few minutes before they followed.

Estelle had been mesmerised by the badger and its light show, but it had still been there when she left and went to the next room. Graham Pierce, Doc Brown, had confirmed her version of events.

It was only when Labby the Cabby entered that Nikki was put on alert. He confirmed the presence of the badger and assured Nikki that it looked exactly the same as it had when he first visited, days before. However, he seemed hesitant when the time came to leave.

"Is there something you want to tell me, Gerald?" Nikki asked kindly, smiling disarmingly as she did so. Gerald was clearly conflicted as he sat back down and wrung his hands.

"Look, I'm not accusing anyone of anything, but I did notice something unusual the other day." He paused and Nikki encouraged him to continue with a raise of her eyebrows.

"Well, we were all impressed when we first saw the artefact, and a few of us took a quick photo on our phones. But Beetlejuice, I don't know his real name, he had this little specialist camera with two lenses. You know, a 3D camera, and he took forever circling the badger taking panoramic pictures, or video. It just seemed odd, that's all."

Nikki began to form a theory. She would need help developing it, but the idea was nestling securely in the back of her mind.

***

The last interviewee of the day was Taylor McCort, a very dapper middle-aged man very much out of character. Nikki assumed he wore a body suit to bulk out his slim frame, when playing Beetlejuice. When he spoke, it became clear that Taylor was a fine actor as his portrayal of the slovenly dressed and potty mouthed character was about as far from reality as it could be.

Taylor recalled entering the room with Labby the Cabby and being there alone for a few minutes before the next staff members came in, complaining about the time he was taking with his photos.

"I adore Hufflepuff, and I adore history, so I wanted to make sure that I had the artefact covered from every angle. After all, when are you going to see a thousand-year-old sculpture again except in the Smithsonian or on a visit to Europe?"

Taylor's answers satisfied Nikki, but only for the time being. Any odd behaviour around the badger could prove to be important at this stage of the investigation.

Nikki gathered her belongings and walked through the Tribute Store towards the exit, which was usually the entrance when the exhibit was open.

As she walked by, she passed a man dressed in overalls bearing a name tag reading John Wojtowicz. It sounded very much like he was cursing under his breath. He recognised her.

"Sorry Nikki, its these damned wax machines. They are supposed to 3D print dinosaurs, dragons, Jaws, you name it, for about $7 each. Most of the time they are fine but every now and again someone gets a shapeless blob. They complain, and John the Waxman is called out, again.

"What happened this time?" Nikki asked, interested.

"Who knows? We're supposed to be printing green dragons this week and someone put in the wrong wax. The dinosaurs are a watery green grey with black bits for good measure.

Apparently, someone, no admissions yet, put the black wax needed for the sorting hat next week into the tank and hey presto, stripey dragons." He paused as he closed the tank lid.

"Shouldn't really complain, though. Most customers quite liked the stripey dragons and didn't even realise anything was wrong. They'll be collectors' items when they're listed on eBay in a year or two. You might want to try one." He laughed at his own joke.

Nikki laughed along with him but declined the offer. She didn't need to see a dodgy green and black striped dragon on her display case beside the 4D glasses and Jaws.

As she drove home Nikki realised, she had acquired a lot of information, and she really hoped that the RixFlixters, the Kids, could help her to make sense of it all.

HARD WORK 2

Saturyaay! Livestream, Universal Orlando, Florida

Pinocchio: Andy, first on as usual.

Andy Giles: That's me, nothing better to do at 10pm UK time on a Saturday night.

Andy Giles had enjoyed an intimate dinner for the first time in, he couldn't remember how long. Now his partner was upstairs getting ready for bed. He was tired too, but he needed to see what was going on 4,000 miles away first.

Luckily Rick had announced a 5pm start in Orlando because Nikki wanted all the Brits and other overseas followers to hear her announcement. Andy waited with bated breath.

Alisha, from Books and Things: Hey Ginger princess, what do you think Nikki will have to say?

Ginger Princess: Don't know. Maybe she is launching her Airbnb. If she is count me in.

Alisha was back at the bookshop counter. She would close soon. It was quiet now, after a busy day. Everyone seemed to be in buying Run Rose Run, by Dolly Parton. Soon she would sit back with a glass of prosecco and enjoy Orlando at night.

She too was intrigued at Nikki's announcement and hoped it would add a little something to her everyday life, something the prosecco didn't.

***

The sun was still out, the sky was still blue, and the Universal Ball was slowly turning in the background. It was also warm, around seventy degrees Fahrenheit, and would probably remain so for the entirety of the livestream. So, Rick and Nikki were wearing tee shirts. Rick was in yellow declaring his love of Mummy Coffee and Nikki was wearing a Hufflepuff tee with a grey body and yellow short sleeves. Rick held the camera high.

"Hi, everyone, welcome to Saturyaay Night at Universal." Nikki waved. "Let's see what's going on in Islands tonight, but first Nikki has an announcement," He paused. "No, she's not pregnant." Nikki shook her head disapprovingly and slapped his arm. "Over to you, Nikki." Rick laughed as he had purposely unsettled her, just for the fun of it.

Ever the stoic professional, Nikki remained composed before the camera.

"Hi everyone. It's supposed to be a secret but, this last week the Hufflepuff Badger was stolen from the Universal Tribute store." There were countless shocked faces around the globe as this news had been supressed by the Theme Park, for obvious reasons. "One way or another, Rick agreed that we, and that means you, too, would try to find the lost Badger and have it restored to its home. I have a picture of the Hufflepuff Badger Sculpture here." She raised a printout showing the old artefact and Rick zoomed in.

Nikki ran through the events that led to the loss and then came her plea.

"We need your help. We can't work this out on our own. If any of you would like to help, or have experience in solving puzzles like this, let Rick know by email. We really do need you."

The livestream progressed as Rick's email inbox gradually filled up.

***

Sunday morning came around quicky and Nikki ran through the emails offering help. She would send out a mass email thanking everyone, but she noticed that she had the makings of a team in the first few emails.

It seemed that they had a real-life Detective on their list. Andy Giles was a Detective Sergeant in the UK. That had to help. He was on the top of the list.

Alisha, from Books and Things, also stood out. She had once been an editor of mystery books for a well-known New York publisher, and anyone who watched Hallmark or Lifetime movies knew that bookshop owners were always good detectives. Perhaps Lea Thompson was available? Nikki discounted the frivolous thought.

Another unexpected find was Ginger Princess, who was a natural puzzle solver and whose puzzle books were never far from her grasp. She also loved Ellery Queen, the master of closed room mysteries, even submitting a couple of her own short stories, yet to be published.

Finally, Darnell Grimes had a CV that included the unpaid role of editor of the online magazine Murder Most Foul, an Agatha Christie fanzine.

Nikki was also intending to ask author JJB to join the team, but he was busy in Qatar with clients and the eight-hour time difference was tricky to manage.

Over the next few hours, whilst Rick was making lunch, Nikki sent a detailed email to Andy, Alsiha, Ginger and Darnell. They now knew as much as she did, and she could relax knowing that some of the weight had been lifted from her shoulders.

She would have given Rick a more prominent role in the search had his second suggestion not been that the badger was potentially carved from a comet, and an alien race had been searching the universe for it for a thousand years, because it was a source of cosmic energy. He was joking of course, at least she hoped so, but it didn't show the level of dedication she needed and needed now.

***

Mr Barrington was busy. He had just met an old friend from the FBI. He needed a favour, and a complimentary day in the parks for the man's family, and a lunch for two at Toothsome's, was a cheap price to pay.

He needed a complete background check on three suspects. They had all checked out on the Universal HR system, but each had an unusual employment history that deserved a deeper search.

Barrington explained what he wanted over Chicken Stroganoff and an impossibly tasty milk shake.

Marilyn Monroe, Labby the Cabby, and Beetlejuice were about to be investigated right back to their high school days by one of the best the FBI could offer; Mark Pietras.

HARD WORK 3

UK, USA, and the RixFlix Universe

Andy Giles sat at his desk. There had been a mugging outside Boots the Chemist and a carjacking five streets away, but his mind was wrestling with the impossibility of the disappearance of the Hufflepuff Badger.

Traditionally a crime needed; means, motive and opportunity. The motive and opportunity were obvious but how was it done? Solve that and the culprit would soon become obvious. He re-examined Nikki's thorough notes.

Six people were in the building, so unless it was an inside job, one of them must have been the thief. Solid lumps of brass do not disappear. Given that anyone would like to benefit from the tens of thousands of pounds, if not hundreds of thousands of pounds, the carving would bring on the black market, all six could be said to have motive.

None of the six people would admit to being in the room but neither could they say emphatically that any other person was in their sight at the time the alarm sounded. So, they all potentially had the opportunity.

No, this was going to be solved by working out how the badger was made to disappear. He started to write up follow-up questions for Nikki to ask the suspects on his behalf.

***

Ginger Princess had read hundreds of closed room mysteries in her life, many even more puzzling than this one. She felt sure that, following her rules, she would find and answer. Her rules for resolving the mystery of an impossibly disappearing object were simple:

1) It was still there, concealed somehow.
2) It had never been there, it just appeared to have been there.

3) It was removed in such a dastardly ingenious fashion that it appeared to be impossible.

After reading the notes from the Tribute Store staff and witnesses, Ginger Princess ruled out 1) and 2). She was totally convinced that she was facing an opponent as clever as Sherlock Holmes and as devious as Moriarty.

But if Ellery Queen had taught her anything, it was to keep an open mind and ask questions. She typed out a list of questions for Nikki to ask back in Orlando.

She was just completing the note when her cell phone rang. It was her dad. He was making his daily call. She smiled and pressed the green phone symbol. Before she could say anything, he spoke:

"Hello, how's my Ginger Princess?" he asked, his voice warm with affection.

***

Alisha of Books and Things had an aura. She didn't know she had an aura, but she did. She was more physically attractive than she believed, and her cleverness, kindness and genial humour attracted customers, male and female. She didn't understand it, perhaps she didn't believe it, but she should have guessed why customers returned time and time again, leaving with any old book as long as she was selling it to them with a smile.

Raymond, a returning customer who was probably in his late fifties had flirted with Alisha shamelessly before deciding to buy a copy of Andy Warhol – Prince of Prints, for his coffee table. As she handed him his new book, she gently squeezed his bare forearm and told him not to leave it so long next time. She didn't see or feel the electric shudder that Raymond felt. There was a book on Salvador Dali that he might purchase tomorrow, he thought as he left, sent on his way with a wave and an Alisha smile.

Alisha turned over Nikki's email in her mind. If an author had sent in this script for proof reading, how would he have explained the impossible theft, and yet maintained credibility. There were many plots that were way out there, but this was real life. The answer would be founded in fact, not fiction. It had to be real.

She thought about the suspicious behaviour of Beetlejuice - could that be a clue? Why did he need so many pictures? Was he going to replicate the object, and replace the original? Probably not, given that the impossible part of the puzzle was the vanishing badger. It was a pity, because that would have been a good plot line.

"I wonder how well they searched Marilyn Monroe," she asked herself out loud in her empty shop. "You could hide anything under those voluminous skirts." Alisha drafted a note to be sent to Nikki and the others, along with a note suggesting that they open an Instagram Group called the Orlando Book Club Mysteries, as they all loved a good book.

***

Darnell Grimes read Alisha's emails and countered with the name Orlando Mystery Club, which was roundly accepted as the group name.

As for the Tribute Store mystery, it was right in his bailiwick (a word he had picked up from one of Agatha Christie's early works). The plot outlined by Nikki in her email, as real as it was, could have been lifted from a Miss Marple novel.

Discounting the possibility that everyone did it together, as Agatha Christie fans would recognise, who was the most likely thief?

Well, following on from period British crime dramas, including those of Agatha, Ngaio Marsh and PD James, it was likely to be the least likely suspect. The one in the background that no-one suspects.

He made an urgent note demanding that Nikki interview Lucy Drake and David Parkin, unassuming and anonymous park attendants, and perfect suspects for this type of caper.

HARD WORK 4

Meanwhile... back at the Tribute Store!

Evan tapped on the door of the Green Room and opened it sufficiently for Nikki to see his perfect smile and his sparkling eyes. She shook herself; she was here on business and Rick was her man. All the same, Evan was very ... decorative.

"I know you're not expecting to speak to me today, but you said if I recalled anything I should share it with you, no matter how irrelevant it may seem?" He made it sound like a question. Nikki nodded. He continued.

"Well, it doesn't come more irrelevant than this, or perhaps more puzzling." He produced what looked like a large pebble. It was smooth, flat on the bottom and domed on the top. It did not describe a circle on plan, it was more of an oval really. Nikki took the piece and noted its weight. It had to be lead and she said so.

"You're right. It's what is called a lead drop, it's the balance of lead left unused from manufacturing. It's just discarded and left to cool. Sometimes they're used for door stops or are attached to string for a vertical plumb bob.

It was found on a shelf in the badger room, and no one can say quite where it came from. I spoke to the room designers and shop artists, but no-one could explain its presence on the shelf.

The best explanation I could find was someone who suggested that it was left behind after Mardi Gras, or even Christmas, as it was so small and black it might easily be overlooked."

Nikki photographed it sitting on her hand, to give it scale, and placed it on the Mystery Club Instagram page.

"Thanks, Evan. You're so sweet." Nikki said sincerely. Evan blushed.

"Well, my little lead blob, what part did you have to play in our little drama?" she asked aloud.

***

Two hours later Nikki met up with Rick at Finnegans. He was ordering Sausages and mash, Colcannon style. Nikki ordered a glass of water and the Leprechaun's Rainbow Salad. Spring break was not a time to go mad and overeat. Summer was just around the corner.

As they ate Nikki contemplated what she had learned. She was certainly grateful to the Mystery Club members for their questions and insights. They each saw the crime differently, and that was a good thing, she hoped.

The email sent out early in the afternoon included information such as:

1) Marilyn Monroe was frisked very well and was more than happy to reveal what was under her voluminous dress.
2) Lucy Drake and David Parkin were two rooms away when the alarm sounded, and they were able to give Marilyn and Doc Brown alibis.
3) Taylor McCort (Beetlejuice) had his bodysuit prosthetics scanned, as they could have easily concealed the badger, but the scan was clear.
4) Labby the Cabby had been scanned and frisked, to no avail, but once again the performer dropped the cat amongst the pigeons. He had seen Beetlejuice come out of the badger room three days before, immediately after the false alarm sounded. "Perhaps that was a dress rehearsal for the real theft," he postulated, shamefaced at suggesting a fellow performer was a criminal.

Nikki sat in the Jeep Wrangler as they drove home. The windows were open, and the roof was off, but the doors were still on. She could see that she was tanning. It showed where her legs had been covered by her shorts. You could get a tan year around in Florida.

"We should have asked for a recovery fee, perhaps a small percentage of the value of the badger," she suggested. It was not cheap keeping a vlog channel running with all of the equipment and software.

"Oh, suddenly you're Thomas Crown! Well, I don't think we have much chance of recovering the badger, especially since SportSec and the Police seem dumbfounded."

Nikki sat quietly. Rick was quite right, of course, but somehow deep inside she felt a little insulted. She was suddenly determined to restore the badger to its glass dome.

***

DS Andy Giles sat in his car, an Audi e Tron S Line, the electric Audi performance saloon he had always promised himself. It cost him over £65,000.00, even after the discounts, but he loved it.

He was parked in a covered car park, waiting for a call to roll out on a raid and checking his email. He had the car read out the email update from Nikki. The software recognised a woman's name in the email header and so used a woman's voice for the narration.

It seemed that Beetlejuice had taken detailed photos and was in the proximity when both alarms sounded. The first could have been a test of the lock down procedures. It made sense when you added the lead drop into the picture. But still, where had the Badger gone on the day? There was still a piece missing for the detective.

He couldn't take it to the prosecutor just yet.

***

Ginger Princess looked at the photo and read the new information about Beetlejuice. An idea was forming. If she was right, it was a brilliant plot, but a brilliant heist was necessary to beat the security team. Ellery Queen was brim full of brilliant plots and so this was familiar ground to Ginger.

***

Alisha had already pegged Beetlejuice as the most likely suspect. Too much evidence pointed in his direction. If she was editing a book, she would have been surprised if it had been anyone else, given the weight of evidence pinning the crime on the striped ghoul.

***

Darnell Grimes had reviewed too many books to not recognise a red herring when he saw one. Beetlejuice was the obvious suspect and therefore it could not be him. It might sound contrary, but it made absolute sense to any Agatha Christie fan.

A SENSE OF JUSTICE 1

On the World Wide Web

Peter, the Potter Collector, was intrigued. He rarely had time to watch other vloggers' creative content on YouTube, but he had recently been in close contact with Rick of RixFlix and so had tuned into Nikki's opening appeal on the livestream.

"Colour me shocked," he had said aloud to an empty room. He had been in Orlando just a few days before for the unveiling of the rare badger, and now it was gone, stolen. Why hadn't they called him in too? After all, he had a Deerstalker in a closet somewhere, from his Sherlock phase, he recalled.

He had tried to push all thoughts of the theft from his mind, but he couldn't. He had to do something. So, he made a number of phone calls. One to his mum - she would look after all things domestic whilst he was away. His brothers, they would pick up and secure any packages he had delivered, and he was expecting some cool boxes this week. Finally, he called American Airlines and booked a flight.

He had a real job as well, of course, but he could easily work from anywhere, at least that was what he told himself and his colleagues. All he had to do now was pack. Now where was that Deerstalker hat?

***

The Zoom meeting began and the whole of the Orlando Mystery Club had signed in.

Nikki was hosting, Andy, Alisha, Ginger Princess and Darnell were all muted, awaiting their turn to speculate on their findings, and the ideas of others. They had all used real backgrounds except Darnell, who had a virtual background showing Universal Studios Archway with people going in and out. It seemed he had the Florida bug bad.

Nikki started the call. Her spring break was slowly ebbing away. Soon she would be back at school and getting up before six in the morning.

"Hi everyone, you are all amazing. I've read your theories and I was stunned by how close they were in explaining the mysterious disappearance.

Let me see if I can bring all of the theories together in one single explanation.

"Someone, possibly Beetlejuice, photographed the badger from every angle. This allowed the suspect to go away and create a 3D virtual model on a computer screen. Then, by setting the size to match the dimensions on the exhibit label, the perpetrator could produce a printable file.

Then using a high-quality 3D printer, they reproduced the badger in plastic, probably making it realistic enough to fool people looking at it through glass."

"It would have taken a few tries but it could be done!" Darnell interrupted. Nikki continued.

"Then they spray painted the model black and added some silver enamel paint to match the marcasite. They may even have glued on some crushed sequins to make it sparkle like the original."

"Then comes the tricky bit," Andy interjected.

"Right." Nikki continued. "They didn't want to be caught on their first attempt and so they did nothing. They just lifted the glass to test security. They got their answer. The doors were locked, and security were at the exhibit inside a minute.

This made the timing as complex as acquiring the replacement model.

Then you all diverge a little. Are we OK so far though?"

Everyone accepted that this must be the case, but each one had doubts.

"OK," Nikki continued. "Alisha and Ginger Princess seem to have a similar idea of how this impossible theft could have happened. Alisha, can you explain? Ginger Princess, jump in as you wish."

Alisha took the floor. Andy and Darnell were soon entranced by the bookseller. She was attractive, yes, but she had that special something. They listened patiently as Alisha's charm washed over them like a summer breeze.

"We believe that the badger was swapped for the 3D printed model by Beetlejuice on the day of the false alarm. From then on everyone was looking at a plastic replica and the real badger was spirited away.

Then on the day of the theft, the perpetrator, Beetlejuice, simply took out the plastic model, crushed it to dust and walked out empty handed, leaving nothing behind but small pieces of broken plastic scattered in the nooks and crannies of the dark exhibit room"

"Ingenious, Alisha, you can see the hand of the 'Ellery Queen' Princess in that explanation, too, but there is a flaw."

Darnell waited until everyone was hanging on his next word. It wasn't an X Factor length pause, but it was close.

"The people in the store at the time of the false alarm were frisked and nothing was found. They were, Labby the Cabby, Beetlejuice – our suspect- and Miss America the wheelchair lady from the entry gate."

"They may have concealed the real one in the room and had someone collect it later, perhaps the next day," Ginger offered. Everyone considered the possibility for a moment.

"No, it doesn't work for me." This time it was Detective Sergeant Andy Giles. "The statement from Mr Barrington clearly states that after the false alarm he lifted the badger and reset it on its pressure pad. He specifically mentions what he calls the 'heft' of the badger, which really means it was heavy. Much heavier than a printed plastic model. He surely would have noticed."

Alisha was quick to address Andy's concern. "Andy, we considered that, and we think we can explain it." She paused to ensure that everyone was listening. The two men most definitely were. "Barrington's colleague, I don't recall his name."

"Evan," Nikki interjected a little too quickly, and blushed.

"Yes, Evan. He discovered a shaped piece of lead. Suppose that it wasn't just a lead drop leftover, suppose it was shaped to fit inside a plastic 3D model, to give it heft!"

"Damn, I forgot about the lead. Well done, ladies. Sometimes with delicate 3D models they are printed in high density plastic, built around a metal former," Andy explained.

"I agree," Darnell added. "But it still doesn't work for me. I have two problems with it. First, the people potentially in the room when the theft took place, or the plastic model was crushed, were all wearing training shoes or sneakers, soft shoes. So, stamping the plastic model to dust was not an option.

And, in the video there was no tool that might have crushed a plastic model to pieces."

"There were a number of things that could have done the job just sitting on the shelves!" Ginger Princess countered. Darnell came back quickly.

"In my experience all props are screwed down or glued in place." Everyone who had been to Universal Studios had at one time or another tried to pick up a prop, only to find it fixed in place. "And, secondly, I still can't get past the fact that they were all frisked after the false alarm, so how did the badger get out of the building?"

The meeting soon reached an impasse, and they were about to reach a conclusion when Nikki remembered her display shelves, filed with Rick's nonsense - sorry, collectibles.

Suddenly, building on the hard work of the Orlando Mystery Club, she knew how the perpetrator had executed their brilliant plan, and how their sleight of hand had misdirected everyone.

Nikki explained her theory to the gathered Zoom meeting, and they all took a sharp intake of breath. The thief's plan had been so brilliantly executed they deserved an award. Someone could write a book about it. Perhaps they would.

A SENSE OF JUSTICE 2

Everyone Loves a Car Chase

Nikki drove faster than she had ever done before, on her way to Universal Studios. She dropped her car in Valet. Rick could reclaim it with his Premier Annual Pass later. She had no time to lose.

She was still out of breath when she arrived at the tiny SportSec office behind the Tribute Store. Her breath didn't come any easier when she opened the door and saw Evan pulling on a clean blue dress shirt over a well-honed but hairless torso. He flashed her a winning smile and she had to wait a second or two before she could speak. After all, she had been running.

Terrence Barrington came into the room just as Evan was fastening his tie. Nikki blushed, realising that he might suspect something had been going on in the tiny office, that clearly had not.

Barrington was too pre-occupied to notice anything other than the paper in his hand.

"This just came through from the FBI in DC, courtesy of an old colleague. It makes interesting reading."

As he lifted his eyes from the document, he could see Nikki was bursting to tell him something.

"Nikki, you go first. My news can wait."

***

"Rick, over here." Rick was shooting a livestream, unaware that Nikki was in the park, as was Peter, The Potter Collector. Rick looked around and spotted Peter, minus his robes but with the curious addition of a Deerstalker.

If Rick was going to be a secret agent/detective, perhaps he should have a Deerstalker hat too, he thought. "Peter, an unexpected pleasure. What brings you to the park?"

"Actually, Nikki does, or at least her mystery does." They took a seat on the bench in the quiet area opposite the Fear Factor and Peter explained his theory as to how the badger was stolen, based entirely on the email he had been copied into by Nikki. All the while anxious RixFlixters around the world listened in as they looked at the static scene on the livestream.

***

Nikki set down her phone. She had half expected Peter, the Potter Collector to email her saying he was on his way, after copying him into the email yesterday, at his request. There was nothing from him in her inbox.

She then proceeded to espouse a theory that was being repeated almost word for word across the park by Peter for the benefit of her husband.

Terrence Barrington listened carefully to the Mystery Club's rather convoluted conclusions, noting that they had the advantage of explaining the facts of the case, or at least most of them. They especially made sense when Nikki revealed her own last-minute contribution.

Suddenly Barrington became animated. This was the first time that Nikki had seen him excited. He was like a little boy again.

"Nikki; Estelle Stevens, Marilyn Monroe and Taylor McCort, Beetlejuice checked out with my contact. However, Gerald Hadley did not.

It seems that Gerald Hadley did not even exist until 2012. Before that there was no social security record, school record or IRS record for the man we know as Hadley. My contact pushed hard to find out why but was pushed back, by the Marshall Service!"

Nikki was clearly expected to understand the relevance of this revelation, but she didn't. Barrington expanded on the finding.

"The Marshall Service re-locates individuals in Witness protection."

Nikki understood immediately.

"So, the reason Labby the Cabby did not show up before 2012 was because the Marshall Service invented our version of Gerald Hadley," Nikki said aloud.

Barrington was pleased with Nikki's quick appraisal of the situation. He continued. "Naturally, the Marshalls are not about to tell us anything about his life pre-2012, but we did a few searches of our own and in the New York newspapers we found a series of articles that we think tell us the story of Gerald Hadley.

"To summarise," Barrington looked over his notes. "Danny The Screwdriver O'Brien was arrested fleeing the scene of a mob hit that went badly wrong. It ended up being the mob that got hit, apparently.

The Feds threatened him with a shopping list of crimes from auto theft to racketeering under RICO regulations. Racketeering became a thing when the Organised Crime Control Act came into force in 1970.

According to my friend, the only things Danny wasn't charged with were the kidnapping of the Lindbergh baby and the murder of Jimmy Hoffa. He was facing a life in a very uncomfortable prison cell, so he testified and was relocated here, presumably. Now using the name Gerald Hadley, for which he has all the necessary government issued papers, he took a job here as Labby the Cabby."

Nikki reached for her phone.

***

When Rick had listened to Peter, he could hardly believe his ears. Labby the Cabby was almost certainly the thief. He had to tell Nikki. He reached for his second phone.

Nikki had the phone to her ear as she and Barrington headed to the staff canteen behind the Esoteric Pictures gates beside Pantages and the Horror Make up Show, to find Labby. Rick picked up.

"It's Labby!" They both said simultaneously, laughing at the exchange.

"Rick, we're heading off to the staff canteen. Can you look in New York?"

"I can, Nikki. I have Peter with me, so we will split up and cover twice the ground. We're on our way. Keep your phone close by."

This was turning into the best livestream ever.

***

Labby the Cabby was sated. He'd had a good lunch and now was heading back to his cab. As he stood holding the exit door, just feet away, on the other side of a black curtain, at the entrance door was the British Security guy and Nikki Cochrane, and they were asking for him by name. There was an urgency in their manner.

He knew instinctively that the game was up. He needed to make a run for it, but how? Presumably security at the exit gates and the staff car park would be alerted by now. So, still wearing his cabby outfit, he jogged over to where the Yellow Cab was standing.

"Damn it!" Labby muttered. Rick was standing by the cab, dressed in yellow, blending in to the old 1946 Plymouth Yellow Cab. Undeterred, Labby ran back to 'Production Central' off Hollywood Boulevard, just by customer service, and entered the door marked "staff only".

Dennis, the storeman, was at the small desk just inside the door. He was the forgotten man of Universal Studios, but he had keys to everything.

"Dennis, can I have the keys to the cab?" Labby asked him. "Some kid has vomited on the paintwork, and I left the cleaning materials in the trunk!"

Dennis handed over the keys, hoping that his services were not required in the clean-up. Who knew what kids had been eating at a theme park.

Labby knew that it was an outside chance, but it was one he had to take. He crept around the cab, unseen by Rick, and slid into the driver's seat, locking the door behind him. There was no central locking in 1946.

Rick heard the door and ran around to the driver's side, but he was too late. The door was locked, and the car engine was being coaxed to life. He rang Nikki and told her what was happening.

***

Nikki ran towards where Labby the Cabby was stealing the cab, leaving Barrington to call security and the Police. She saw the cab driving along just as she reached Marilyn Monroe, sitting posing for photographs on her silver Cadillac.

***

Peter, the Potter Collector, also had a call from Rick. He couldn't believe that Labby was stealing the cab. Where on earth would he go? As luck would have it, he found himself standing outside Transformers, where Doc Brown was posing for pictures with a Back to the Future 2 DeLorean.

"Doc, I need a word." Graham Pierce the Doc Brown actor listened carefully as Peter explained.

"Doc," Peter asked, "How would he get out of Studios in the Yellow Cab? Surely the park is sealed up." Staying in character for the gathering crowd, Graham put his palm to his head and said: "Great Scott! I'll wager he's heading for the gates beside the New York skyline."

"Does this car actually run?" Peter asked, nodding towards the DeLorean.

"You betcha!" Doc responded. "I've been driving it around all day. Hop in." They both climbed into the car and the gull wings closed. Peter was in heaven; this was quite possibly the best day of his life.

***

Rick was mad at himself as much as at Labby. He had allowed the man to make a run for it, albeit at ten miles per hour through crowds of park goers, parting the way before him and waving and cheering him along.

Rick jogged along after him, not knowing what he would do if he caught him up. The livestream was continuing as he ran, bumpy pictures but exciting. The internet was alive with Instagram, Facebook and twitter messages about a real-life chase at Universal Studios. Was it real, or was this some kind of show? The livestream number were up from 500 to over 800 already.

***

Nikki attracted Marilyn's attention. "Estelle, Labby is the one who stole the badger, and he's making a run for it in the Yellow Cab. Can we chase after him?"

"Of course we can, Honey! Climb in."

"Estelle, this car isn't built for chasing anything. It never leaves the park," Chuck, the driver noted. "Oh Chuck, honey, this is our chance to make it big. Just drive." She turned to Nikki, still as Marilyn, and said, "Boys! They are supposed to be the reckless ones. Let's show 'em!"

The Cadillac drove onto New York, and they spotted Labby in the distance. He had parted the crowds for them. The impromptu veteran car parade proceeded onwards, park guests waving and cheering, not understanding what was really going on

***

Rick was missing out; he could see Labby disappearing, with Marilyn giving chase, and now the DeLorean was tucking in behind. He had an idea.

The Blues Brothers were idling their car, just around the corner from their usual show spot outside Finnegan's, when that yellow shirted vlogger jumped into the backseat.

"Hey buddy, you can't be in here, it's against the rules," Jake protested. "When did we ever follow rules?" Ellwood asked. Rick explained what was going on, urging them to follow the thieving cabby.

There was a moment's hesitation, and then the car burst into life and screeched away down the street to give chase.

**

Universal's star handlers were standing in a group throwing their hands in the air. Was everyone going mad? What was happening? Who on earth did they call for a breach of protocol as serious as this?

"What's going on?" asked Maxwell Greer, aka Shaggy. A staff member explained about the impromptu parade-cum-chase and without missing a beat, Shaggy jumped into the Mystery Machine and started it up.

The star handlers yelled No in unison, all to no avail.

"All we need now is for Murph to steal Hagrid's Motorbike and we will have lost every vehicle on the plot!" their supervisor yelled. "Do something!"

A SENSE OF JUSTICE 3

Believe Your Eyes.

Labby drove down past the big stage and the Jimmy Fallon ride before turning sharp left at the New York Skyline. He had ben astonished at the way the parkgoers cleared the way for him, clapping, waving and cheering as he passed. As far as they were concerned this was a show, but where he was concerned it was a getaway.

As he turned left, he faced a timber wall with a personnel gate at the side. It looked impenetrable for the average onlooker, but he knew that these giant gates had been used in the past to bring in Christmas trees and Halloween props. He pushed the heavy '46 Plymouth right up to the gate and then moved forwards very slowly. There was resistance at first, but then the bolt sprung as the screws gave way and the gates burst open.

As he drove through, he could see the immediate right turn onto the fire road that led to the maintenance staff car park on Studio Drive. He made good progress along Ironside Drive and then McHale Navy Drive before emerging onto Universal Studios Plaza.

A left turn onto the dual carriageway road took him to Turkey Lake Road, heading towards Sand Lake Road. Now that he was on a proper carriageway, he could floor the accelerator and see what the old car could do on a proper road. He pushed down on the gas pedal, and nothing happened. The old car eventually crept up to 35 miles per hour but would do no more.

He should have guessed that they would put limiters on those cars that were exclusively used in the parks. Still, he only needed to get to the 528, head towards the airport and he could dump the old car at any exit. Unfortunately, at these speeds that might take forever.

***

Peter, the Potter Collector and Doc Brown were hot on Labby's tail as he exited onto Turkey Lake Road. Their vehicle was also speed restricted, but Doc was managing to get some acceleration out of the old car, at least until it reached 55 miles per hour. He turned to Peter, who was charged with keeping Labby in view and spoke.

"When this baby hits eighty-eight miles per hour, you're going to see some serious stuff!"

Peter was glad of the expurgated version of the famous phrase; it was a family friendly car chase, after all.

They were on Labby's tail as he flung the old taxi left onto Sand Lake Road. Peter grew concerned.

"Doc, if he gets into heavy traffic, we could lose him. We have the faster car, why don't we get ahead of him and force him to stop?"

"No, Peter, he's driving a heavy 46 Plymouth and we're driving a DeLorean, he would tear through us like tin foil!" Doc responded, still maintaining character.

"Yes, I was forgetting about the tin foil quote," Peter lamented.

***

Close behind the DeLorean came another heavy car, the sleek Cadillac convertible carrying Marilyn Monroe and Nikki. Maybe they could get ahead of the Yellow Cab and force it to stop. Sadly, their vehicle was travelling at its top speed of 45 miles per hour, so whilst it wasn't gaining ground, it wasn't losing ground either.

Marilyn and Nikki urged Chuck on, but he was already doing the best he could, and feeling a tad overdressed in a suit and tie in the warm sunshine.

***

Rick was having a little more luck. The old Crown Victoria ex Police Car, with all of its graffiti, was moving very quickly, but it was also belching out diesel fumes and smoke like an old factory chimney.

"Ellwood, take a left here, then right at the next turn, and we can take a short cut along Universal Boulevard and be at Sand Lake Road West first."

Rick knew the roads to Epic Universal well, and had assumed that Labby would head towards the airport, given that he turned down Turkey Lake Road and not up.

"If you say so, Rick," Ellwood said, enjoying himself as Jake cranked the old radio up to full volume.

***

The two patrolmen sitting at the junction on Sand Lake Road watching the traffic from their patrol car were bored. Theirs was a thankless task. The driver, a Sergeant of long standing, was closing in on retirement. The rookie at his side was in his twenties, eager and restless.

They both had to take a second look at the cavalcade of cars that had flashed through the lights as they were turning red. The rookie picked up the radio and was ready to broadcast back to the station house when the older man took the radio handset and placed it back on its cradle.

"What are you doing, son?" he asked. "I'm calling it in. Another car could intercept them at the next junction."

 The older man shook his head.

"I don't think so. You radio into HQ that a 1940's New York Yellow Taxicab just ran a red light whilst being pursued by Marilyn Monroe in a silver Cadillac, the Blues Brothers, Doc Brown in a DeLorean and Shaggy and Scooby Doo in the Mystery Machine, and we will be spending the next three months in psych evaluations. Let's leave it to the State Troopers." His manner and tone left no room for discussion.

On the much quieter Universal Boulevard Labby could see his problem in the rear-view mirror. On his rear bumper was Marilyn Monroe, and behind her came the Blues Brothers with Doc Brown coming up on the outside lane. But ahead of them all and almost level with the Yellow Cab, that Rick insisted on calling Maxi the Taxi, was a bright yellow van. The Mystery Machine. Worse still, at the wheel was that punk kid who was always so loud in the canteen. He was still in character as Shaggy.

"What did I do to deserve this?" Labby muttered under his breath.

***

Damien, who once won a Hollywood place at the Orlando heat of American Idol, stroked his false beard. He was Shaggy now; Damien was being subdued under 1970's flares and a tight top. What would Shaggy do, he asked himself as the van drew level with Labby's cab. Actually, he knew exactly what Shaggy would do if he suffered the abuse that Damien suffered when posing as Shaggy for photos. OK, so most people were polite and friendly, adoring even, but there were some who absolutely were not. He always had to simply smile politely in response. He grimaced and growled. He wished he had a dollar for every time some kid shouted out, "it's the caretaker in a mask, dumbass!".

Immediately up ahead he could see Icon Park, the home of the Coca Cola wheel and the slingshot. Damien put his foot down, the van responded and as soon as he was ahead of the cab he braked, hard.

***

Labby had no option; a collision was inevitable if he didn't react. He didn't trust the stopping power of 70-year-old brakes, especially without a seatbelt.

He braked and spun the wheel. Power steering would have helped, turning into the Icon Park parking lot. He almost came to a halt as the car stalled. He had almost forgotten he was driving a stick shift. The cars behind him had to react as well, and they did.

***

"Block off the entrance to the multistorey car park, Chuck!" Nikki yelled as she saw the Yellow Cab stall. Chuck swung left and then right, parking the Cadillac across the road in the parking lot that led to the multistorey entrance.

Immediately behind the Cadillac were the Blues Brothers with Rick, still filming for the livestream, acting as back seat driver. "Go left!" he shouted at Ellwood, who finished the thought for him. "I know, we cut off his route back to the Boulevard."

There were now over a thousand people on the livestream and Channel 9 were rebroadcasting it live from the internet.

At the back of the cavalcade, Peter urged Doc Brown to close up the gap behind the Yellow Cab, the three vintage cars leaving Labby nowhere to go.

Rick, Nikki and Peter jumped out of their respective cars, Peter after waiting a painfully long time for the gull wing door to reach full height, and ran to the cabby's door.

***

It was over now. Labby could see that now. He unlocked the door, opened it and stepped out, handing the keys to Rick.

"Labby, how could you do this? We have hung out together so often at the parks."

The livestream numbers were close to two thousand now and YouTube were having to switch servers to cope.

Labby had the good manners to look shamefaced. "It was a chance to get away from the parks and grab myself a new life. Pina Coladas, the beach and some handsome ladies." He looked at Nikki and winked. She blushed again.

Peter took the keys out of Rick's hand.

"I have an idea where the badger may be," he said excitedly. "Did you wonder why Labby made a run for it in the cab?" No-one had. "The truth is he could have changed clothes and blended into the crowds. As a staff member he probably knows a hundred ways out of the park without going through the guest exit and we could never cover them all." He paused. "And he must have known that."

Nikki twigged immediately. "He took the cab because he needed the cab, or at least, he needed what's in the cab."

Labby looked defeated but he was keeping his own counsel.

Rick searched the interior but found nothing. Peter popped the trunk and saw only the spare wheel in an immaculately clean space. Peter looked disappointed.

"Wait. Help me lift the spare wheel," Nikki urged. The two of them lifted the spare from the shaped well as Rick filmed, and were left with the jack, a tyre iron and an almost invisible black canvas bag bearing the Plymouth logo and which at one time may have carried lug nuts or some other spares.

Nikki lifted out the bag, with Rick and Peter standing beside her so closely as to be restricting her arm movement. Everyone was excited.

By the time she opened the bag and lifted out the bubble wrapped Hufflepuff Badger, which really did have heft, she was being closely observed by the weirdest gang in history. As she turned to show everyone the badger, she could see in the informally arranged semicircle: Marilyn Monroe, The Blues Brothers, Doc Brown and Shaggy from Scooby Doo.

And Rick was capturing it all on video! There had to be a Pulitzer Prize in his future, surely.

Labby could have made a run for it on foot, but he was not a runner, not even a jogger. He could do a fast walk, but only for a couple of hundred yards, and that just wouldn't cut it.

The game was up and Peter, the Potter Collector, posed for a group photo, regretting that he had left his Deerstalker hat in the DeLorean.

A SENSE OF JUSTICE 4

The Denouement.

Terrence Barrington sat with Rick, Nikki, Peter and Labby the Cabby at a picnic table in the shadow of the Star Flyer. Universal Security were escorting the show cars and their occupants back to the Studios, complaining that not one vehicle was Florida State roadworthy or insured!

Later the performers involved would have to face an HR disciplinary hearing, but what could the good and great in management do? They needed their cast members, and, after all, the actors had restored the badger to the exhibition, saving the Orlando Theme Park managers a huge insurance claim. Terrence Barrington was sure they would get off with a stern talking to and a half day of responsibility retraining.

***

"Gerald, stop me if I go wrong," Barrington asked. He had assured the witness protectee that the Marshalls were keen to keep this fiasco out of the Press, having spent tens of thousands of dollars relocating him in the first place. Labby the Cabby would probably spend no time in prison but would spend the rest of the year in community service or clearing rubbish from the I-4 median, wearing a DOC coverall.

"I have to thank Andy Giles, Alisha, Ginger Princess and Darnell Grimes, the Orlando Mystery Club, and of course, Nikki." Barrington directed attention to his new best friend with a flourish of his hand, a gesture that seemed foreign to him and his British manners.

"This is what we believe happened."

The three vloggers listened intently.

"Labby took photos of the exhibit and then, for misdirection, pointed us in the direction of Beetlejuice. He took his photos and created a virtual

3D model from them. There are a number of Artificial Intelligence Drawing programmes on the web that will do the trick.

With the 3D imagery he was able to print a 3D model of the badger - not in plastic as the club members thought, but in wax. He had lifted a tin of green wax from the Studios storeroom. This was the wax used in various outlets for printing Sharks, Dinosaurs etc.

He sprayed the green wax with a thin coating of matt black vinyl spray paint and finished it with shiny costume jewellery shards to replicate the Marcasite. It was quite heavy, but not heavy enough, and so he weighted it with the lead drop we found.

On the day of the supposed false alarm, he stole the real badger and replaced it with the fake. We had experienced glitches when setting up, and so when we saw the badger safely in place, we frisked everyone leaving and left it at that."

"So, how did he smuggle the badger out?" Nikki asked.

"I think I can help there," Peter interjected. "He was right behind Miss America in her wheelchair, which doesn't go through the metal detector, for good reason. I'm guessing that he secured the badger somewhere under her seat whilst it was dark in the Tribute Store and recovered it later, after she was frisked and cleared."

"It's true," Labby spoke for the first time. "I stuck it to the underside of the plastic seat pan with double sided tape. Unfortunately, as soon as she was cleared, she raced off down the street to start a shift at the gate. I eventually caught her up and said she was trailing my scarf behind her as it had become snagged in her wheelchair frame. She allowed me time to free it. I released the badger, pocketed it and she went off, none the wiser."

"Then on the day of the theft," Barrington continued, "Labby hid behind a curtain until the room was empty and then lifted the glass pyramid cover, took the wax badger and closed the lid with the alarm sounding.

It took us around 45 seconds to get to the case, during which time Labby extricated the lead drop weight and then dropped the wax badger into the liquid wax tank that printed the 3D dragons, at the back of the room. Then he hid behind the curtain again, cleaned the wax off the lead and joined the crowd looking at the empty case.

After some careful examination of the blackout curtains, we found deposits of green and black wax."

"That explains why some of the dragons were a greyish green or had black stripes!" Rick concluded. Everyone nodded.

"Then, when we searched the visitors and the Tribute Store there was nothing to find, except the lead drop weight. The replica had long since melted into the wax tank.

We had the tank emptied a little while ago and found remnants of costume jewellery and sequins in the bottom of the tank."

Peter, the Potter Collector, clapped ironically. "Genius, Labby, absolute genius." The others looked impressed too.

Thinking of Ginger Princess and her predilection for crime stories, Nikki remarked, "If this doesn't make the pages of Ellery Queen, I don't know what will."

There was laughter all around the table until the Orlando Police placed handcuffs on Labby the Cabby.

EPILOGUE

A Few Days Later.

Orlando Sentinel

Metro Section – Staff Reporter

Ancient Artefact Restored to HP Exhibition!

After a strange, some would say surreal, car chase through the International Drive area of Orlando, an ancient artefact, said to date back to the Saxon kings of England circa 990CE, was discovered in the back of a classic car.
The Police, Universal Security and private security contractor SportSec are keeping very quiet on the circumstances of the loss and the recovery.
However, this reporter followed the unusual car chase on Channel 9 news, and on a video livestream from RixFlix. I am told by a source close to the vloggers that a theme park employee had made off with the artefact in some kind of protest against exhibiting ancient relics for entertainment. RixFlix is a YouTube Channel that broadcasts regular park updates and is fronted by a couple called Rick and Nikki.

Rick set down the newspaper and answered the door. A minute later he arrived in the lounge with two Winter Garden Pizza Company pizza boxes in a DoorDash bag.

They would be sharing an 18" Winter Garden Deluxe and a 14" Margherita.

Courtney was out doing those things young adults do when they offer their parents the vague answer, "I'm going out", having been asked what they are doing tonight. That meant the couple were finally alone together. No editing, no serial killers or international art thieves.

Just Rick, Nikki, Pizza and not a yellow tee shirt in sight. Nikki snuggled into Rick as they sat folding and eating pizza. As she did so, she noticed –

with a sigh – that the Shrek 4D glasses were back on her shelves. But tonight, was not the time to address that.

They were reliving their first date.

As the Universal globe appeared on the large TV screen and the accompanying bass drum beat reverberated around the surround system, Rick made an observation.

"We are less than halfway through the year, and we've already apprehended a serial killer and a major art thief."

The opening credits appeared on the screen for the 1991 film, "The People Under the Stairs", courtesy of their 4K Blue Ray DVD. The years began to roll back.

Rick finished his thought before the film got going.

"If all this happened at a peaceful time of year, imagine what might happen at Halloween."

They both laughed, but ultimately events in October would show that they had laughed a little too soon.

Original Cover Art

J JACKSON BENTLEY

DON'T GO ALONE!

A RixFlix Hallowe'en Short Story

Edited by Susan Whitfield, Vice President, RixFlix

Published by Fidus USA
An imprint of www.FidusPress.com

All rights reserved. This is a work of fiction. Real world places, characters, and companies are re-imagined and used in a fictitious setting throughout. No similarity to actual real-life characteristics, actions or behaviours is intended. The cooperation and permissions of Rix Flix and its named owners, subscribers and followers is appreciated and applauded by the author. All proceeds to Rix Flix and Road trips Channels.

Copyright J Jackson Bentley 2022

Hallowe'en is supposed to be scary but when Rick and Nikki are invited to a private event hosted by a witch in Slytherin Robes, they should have spotted trouble ahead. Slytherin is represented by a snake.

"Bodacious stunts and awesome surprises take you on a trick or treat through time."

Bill and Ted's Halloween Adventure 1992

1

San Bernadino Federal Correction Facility, California. USA.

Ingrid Carmody stood outside the brutalist modern prison, all concrete and wire. No soft edges. She dabbed at her moist eyes, trying to avoid mascara run, and the never fashionable Panda look. She had just visited her fiancé, they had met and become engaged whilst he was in federal prison and so it was probable that they would never marry, sleep together or even hug.

Life was so unfair. She had first met the man of her dreams when he had already been tried and convicted of murder, kidnapping, and other crimes. Crimes for which he bore no real responsibility. He was a genius, a man ahead of his time. Such men had peccadillos, but we needed such men, in her twisted opinion. If a few worthless people lost their lives so that such men could thrive and save the world, then so be it. There were three hundred and fifty million people in the USA; the country could afford to lose a few, so that a great man, a strong man, could satisfy his needs and still lead America and the World.

Her fiancé could have been great. He would have been great, but for two ordinary people who had stood in his way, two unexceptional people who had – by rank good fortune – brought him down.

This was a democracy. How could two common people have the gall to derail the man who would not just be the next President of the United States of America, but the greatest President of the United States? And when he took the Oath of Office, she would have happily stood by his side, a quiet but determined First Lady.

Carswell Lawrence Judd needed to be avenged, and she had proven since childhood that she was just the lady to wreak havoc in the lives of those ordinary people who stood in her way.

2

Dionysus Biotech Inc. Santa Barbara. California.

Dillon Carmody looked down from his sixth-floor office onto the plaza below. The company driver had just delivered his sister back to the office from her weekly visit to the madman who was now her fiancé. She stepped out of the Lexus and looked up; it was as if she knew he would be watching. He shivered. She could not see him through the mirrored building envelope, but she made eye contact all the same. Her green eyes penetrating to his very soul, as they always had.

He loved his sister; he looked after her. She was special and always had been. From being a toddler, she had been eccentric, or as the neighbours said, strange. Her off-beat personality was not helped by her unusually asymmetric face; one side had always appeared to be stretched out and slightly higher than the other. It was not helped by the presence of a faded childhood scar running horizontally across her cheek. Despite the fact that most boys at school had described her as plain, at best, she had her admirers.

Gavin Collison, for example, had pursued her his whole life. He loved her mind, her quirky humour and her absolute absence of social etiquette. She was five feet ten inches tall and very slim, the doctors said unhealthily thin, but she disagreed. She ate like a horse but somehow the weight stayed off. Perhaps it would catch up with her later in life.

Dillon was a dollar billionaire, as was his sister, but it wasn't his doing. He was a competent businessman, he had done very well at Harvard Business School, but Ingrid was a flawed genius.

They worked together in the same large office. She always wanted to be close to him. They even shared a house in the hills. A house that might more accurately be described as an estate.

In 2015 *Dionysus* had been a small biotech company surviving largely on research grants from other companies and working for government departments. Then came the breakthrough that Ingrid had been working on since childhood - Vocatusil.

Dillon and Ingrid had been raised by parents who enjoyed a comfortable middle-class lifestyle. Dad was a dentist, Mom was a life coach, but their young lives were blighted by alcohol abuse in the home. Their parents kept their alcoholism a secret from others, even their own siblings, but at home they would drink themselves into a stupor. They would become violent and abusive to each other and, unfortunately, their children.

The next morning apologies died out after a few months. They were worthless anyway, but Dillon tried his level best to protect his sister. Most of the time he succeeded, and she loved him for it. Theirs was a bond beyond that of normal siblings. Theirs was a sibling love that rivalled any in Greek tragedy.

Then, one terrible night, a wineglass was thrown and Ingrid's cheek was sliced open. Despite their wealth the couple had the wound closed at a local medical clinic where they were not known to the staff. The faded botched stitching scar was still visible today.

Vocatusil was a drug designed to replace alcohol for addicts. It came in various doses to allow intervention at any stage of addiction, and to allow the slow process of dependency reduction to take place naturally.

Named after the Latin word for alcohol, it was the counterpart to the ironic company name, chosen by Ingrid, whose dark sense of humour knew no limits. Dionysus being the Greek god of wine, the Roman equivalent being Bacchus.

***

Ingrid imagined her brother looking down at her from their office. He was a beautiful man, his features were pleasing to the eye, but it was his sweet nature that she loved. He had always protected her, and he always would. She needed to know that someone out here in the world cared for her enough to die for her.

Deep down Ingrid fully understood that her new fiancé would not have given her a second glance outside of the prison environment. The women who had been on his arm at galas, political rallies and the Oscars were famous for their beauty, if for nothing else.

None of this mattered to Ingrid. She loved him, and she would avenge him, whilst simultaneously funding endless appeals in the courts. Carswell Lawrence Judd did not deserve to be in prison, and the people who put him there deserved to be punished.

Rick, Nikki, watch out! I am coming for you! she muttered under her breath.

3

RixFlix Manor, Winter Garden, Orlando. USA.

Things were all quiet in the pleasantly appointed house that Rick and Nikki called home. The Airbnb annexe, the in-law suite, was unoccupied, a rarity these days, and this allowed the couple to be themselves. The annexe had been rented out almost nonstop since the first guests arrived way back when Rick and Nikki were still tracking down the Hoogflpaff badger.

There had been lessons to learn from their guests and their foibles, but all in all it had proven to be a great success, and the income helped to cover the household bills for the impressive five bedroomed property in this desirable sub-division with its own lake. It also gave the family, and mini-Winnie, the Labrador puppy, somewhere to stay independently, when visiting.

Rick sat back in the hot tub and relaxed. Hs had been a hard morning, walking around Universal videoing and creating content. Nikki may have disputed this view of life, working as she did with children who have life challenges, often for up to 10 hours a day.

Rick's tablet pinged; he had a message. He opened the folder, being careful to keep the tablet away from the water. He didn't need another water-based incident. The message was addressed to him and Nikki jointly. It was an invitation. It read:

"We are previewing a haunted house for HHN, in the old Hard Rock Café location in Universal Studios. We are seeking opinion from HHN regulars before we develop the attraction further. It is hoped that we will find a permanent home, year-round, for the attraction in the form of a Halloween themed escape room. We are in advanced talks with a major theme park but are not allowed to discuss any plans as yet.

We would like you to be the first of our focus group to tour. All will be theme park vloggers acquainted with HHN. The reason we wanted to ask you specifically is that the theme for the first HHN escape room is: The People Under the Stairs. Can you escape the hungry children?

We read in a recent short story how it was your first movie together as a couple and we wanted to make it special.

If you are interested send a text to the number below and you will receive instructions by text, as to how to access the preview. You will both need active annual passes or park passes.

Iris Coulthard, EscapetoEntertainment Inc.

Rick knew that Nikki would be on board with his decision and so he texted back within minutes, saying they would be delighted to attend.

Within five minutes he had to set down his mocktail - can't afford to dehydrate in Florida - to open a second message from his new friend Iris.

"Welcome aboard Rik and Nikki, here are the instructions on how to access the house preview."

Attached was a set of instructions along with a QR code. The code could be printed or shown electronically. Rick and Nikki were going to see a Haunted House the day HHN began. This was a scoop for RixFlix. There had to be a video or two in this.

Rick loved Halloween; it was his favourite time of year at the parks. He sank back in the hot tub, sipped on his drink, and daydreamed of *The People Under the Stairs*.

***

Water on the newly painted deck alerted Nikki to the fact that her beloved husband had been in the hot tub whilst she was at work. Oh, how she also wanted to be a full time RixFlix employee. She might even find time to sleep.

Rick was editing in the ground floor studio that had been described as a separate diner on the house plans when they bought it. Nikki collapsed into her own office chair. She didn't want to unload her workload burdens on her husband, he was too easily distracted as it was. So, she simply asked him what was happening.

Rick's smile was wider than usual. That usually meant one of three things; a new instalment of the Zelda game was due, a new favourite food had arrived at Universal, or Epic Universe was scheduled to open unexpectedly early.

Rick simply responded by showing Nikki the invitation to the HHN House preview. Soon, Nikki was grinning, too.

The People Under the Stairs might not be everybody's idea of a first date movie, but it was their first movie, and that meant everything. Nikki read the invitation and asked Rick about the company involved. He explained that he had been busy and had not looked at their website, but he was sure it was fine. They would have a great night.

Nikki clicked on the link to *EscapetoEntertainment.com* and found herself at a professionally curated site that explained the history of the company and its various forays into the entertainment world. Most impressive was its alleged links to major companies whose products ranged from comic books to Hollywood films.

Flattered that the company head of creative enterprises, Iris Coulthard, had been interested in RixFlix enough to research them on the internet and read the books, Nikki decided it would be rude to refuse the invitation, knowing very well that 'click bait Rick' would have already responded for them both.

Now was the time to relax. A change of clothes and one of Rick's speciality dinners, were on the cards, before sitting in front of a computer for a few more hours.

Universal Studios Orlando,
HHN 31, Night 1, 2022

Rick and Nikki simply loved Halloween Horror Nights at Universal Studios, Orlando. Rick had still been a young adult when Halloween Horror Nights had begun here in 1991, under the name Fright Nights. Since then, what had begun as a three-night event on October 25, 26, and 31, 1991, with just one haunted house, *The Dungeon of Terror*, had grown exponentially. In 1991, for only $12.95 you could be scared out of your wits by the haunted house and numerous scare actors.

The next year the event was wisely renamed "Universal Studios Florida Halloween Horror Nights" and was advertised as being the second annual Halloween Horror Nights. This time there were two haunted houses, with The Dungeon of Terror returning to the Jaws queue building, and *The People Under The Stairs* making its debut in Soundstage 23.

It was, therefore, inevitable that an invitation in 2022 to preview a re-imagined Haunted House, based under their seminal date movie, would be accepted.

The couple had spent many happy hours being frightened and scared witless on the streets of Universal Studios. They were terrified by the antics in the haunted houses, and they laughed until they cried with Bill and Ted's Excellent Halloween Adventures.

Tonight, they were meeting with another Vlogging couple who posted in the name Lording it in Florida, Lucy Lord leading the way. It was to be a crossover event. Sadly, the invitation to the preview of the People Under the Stairs house was only for Rick and Nikki. Nonetheless, the Lords could easily occupy themselves elsewhere in the park whilst awaiting Rick and Nikki's return. The Lords would be excited to hear, albeit second hand, exactly what the preview was like.

It was certainly going to be a day to remember, but potentially for very different reasons.

***

The plan was simple enough. Rick and Nikki would meet the Lords in Citywalk at 11am. They would plan the crossover event in their heads, who would be filming what and when. Then they would go into the park, forget all of their plans and wing it.

It was always a thrill passing under the great golden archway, having just passed the ever-spinning Universal Ball. The colourful giant medallion above their heads proclaimed that HHN 31 was upon them.

They walked through the park together taking snippets of video, noting that the streets were dressed for Halloween but that some exhibits were covered by tarpaulins, to shield the more gruesome exhibits from the sensitive eyes of the daytime visitors, and children.

The small group were in Central Park discussing the rest of the day when Nikki realised that Rick had disappeared. This had been a very strange year for the couple and for a moment she was concerned. Then out of the corner of her eye she saw a bright yellow tee shirt at the Crepe stand. A minute later Rick arrived with a crepe stuffed with cream, raspberries and blueberries. Nikki glared at him.

"What?" he said defensively, registering the disapproval. "It might be a long filming session. We could miss lunch." Nikki shook her head. She almost said "When have you ever missed lunch?" but she held her tongue. Rick wasn't listening anyway; his full attention was fixed on how to eat his Crepe without coating his yellow tee shirt in fruit sauce.

"OK, Nikki, Rick. We will meet you back here at 1:30pm if we don't get a text earlier. That should give you plenty of time in the preview," Lucy Lord said, looking at her watch. The two couples parted.

A Private Event

Rick and Nikki were excited. They turned left out of the cultivated garden that was labelled Central Park and passed the busy pin trading stand before heading to the very back of the park, as they been instructed on the email.

Excitable children were noisily running rings around exhausted adults as they argued about what to do first in the Kids Zone. As Rick and Nikki walked by, they smiled, recalling taking pictures of their own girls right there, in front of Woody Woodpecker.

As they traversed the area they bore left until they arrived in front of a standard Universal sign reading: Private Event. A smiling man in a suit and tie, despite the heat, stood blocking the entrance. He said nothing as Rick approached. Eventually Rick realised that he would have to produce some evidence that he was being invited to the Private Event.

He handed over a paper copy of an email which had a printed pass on its face. The man scanned the QR code and then stepped aside. He had still not spoken a word; he was obviously in character. What Rick and Nikki did not know was that Jerome, the large African American gatekeeper was as much in the dak as they would soon be. He had been hired by an agency to guard the entrance and allow just two people into the event, Rick and Nikki.

He had puzzled over the assignment, but it paid three hundred bucks, and his wife and two kids had been given complimentary passes to the park/ It was a good gig. In a few minutes he would place his jacket, shirt and tie in a locker and walk the park in his white tee shirt and dress pants. Not ideal, but he would still have fun, then he would be back to his second security job at the park entrance tonight, checking oddly dressed young adults for drugs and weapons.

***

Rick and Nikki walked along the heavily shadowed path. The shrubbery on either side of them was a little overgrown, and they soon moved into the area that once accommodated the Hard Rock Café. Of course, that was demolished eleven years ago, and the new 'back of lot' utility plot was now mostly empty. The marquee standing on the lot was occasionally used as a haunted house at Halloween, but not this year.

The doorway was plain and unadorned, industrial almost. A laminated notice was posted on the door, which read "Come on in…. if you dare!". When Rick pushed open the door they found themselves in a dark, black curtained space, illuminated with black lighting. The only spotlight in the space shone on a vintage poster of The People Under the Stairs movie; the poster dated from 1991.

They were looking at the poster and wondering what to do next when there was a puff of smoke and, seemingly from nowhere, appeared a tall witch dressed in a Slytherin robe and a witch's hat bearing the image of a coiled snake in a coat of arms. The green eyes of the snake seemed to shine and glare at the couple.

In a theatrical witch voice, the tall woman said: "Aah, a Hufflepuff and a Gryffindor, visiting my haunted house. Are you brave enough to join the people under the stairs? If you are: Beware of the children, they are hungry." Instead of cackling she appeared to speak Parseltongue.

Then, from behind the curtain she theatrically produced two tumblers filled with a green liquid which had jelly babies floating in the cocktail. "Murph, the Magical One, has created this special drink to give you courage and calm your nerves," she said, using her witch voice, as she handed the luminous drinks to the unsuspecting vloggers. They relaxed; the preview was about to begin, and they both knew very well that Murph made exquisite mocktails.

Then in a normal voice she gave a disclaimer: "Under park rules I am obliged to tell you that this is the alcohol free 'friendly' version."

Rick and Nikki drank the delicious cocktails down quickly and then ate the jelly babies. A moment of madness they would regret later.

Zelda: The Return of the Hero

Rick dreamed that he was watching himself, as if in a movie. The version of Rick he was watching was sleeping. He was lying down flat in a shallow stone sarcophagus. Water was draining away from around him, but this other Rick did not appear to be wet.

"Open your eyes," a disembodied voice ordered. Rick did so and was immediately transported into the body he had been watching, his own body. To be precise the body he now occupied was enhanced. He appeared to be younger, had well defined abs, and best of all his hair was visible below his cap.

"Rick, arise and come to me. I am in the column of Eslin".

Rick sat up and looked around the otherwise empty cave. The walls were dry and appeared to be naturally formed. There was no sign of tools being used to create the space. Rick swung his legs around until they dangled over the edge of the uncomfortable bed and clambered down from the stone edifice onto a dusty stone floor. As he looked around, he found himself facing a giant stylised eye sculpture. The eye carved into the top of the column appeared to be highlighted in neon. The eye sculpture was tilted at a thirty-degree angle atop the stone column.

Rick soon came to understand that when the voice spoke the eye turned blue, then, when it fell silent there was no light. Rick somehow already understood that this eye carried the voice of the spokesperson for the *Realm*, the council who maintain harmony on all outer worlds. Including the Kingdom of Hyrule.

He didn't remember how he knew this, but he was now twenty years younger, had an impressive six pack and a full head of hair, so he wasn't going to start asking questions. The eye lit up.

"You have a task that is so important that your failure will doom the whole of Hyrule." Rick was confused. The immediate situation felt real enough but he was standing in a cave and the world beyond the cave opening was, quite honestly, a cartoon like rendering. To be accurate the view from the cave was exactly like the landscape that had been depicted in the video games he had played decades before, but in 4K. He reached up to scratch his head, forgetting there was a full head of blond hair falling to his shoulders. He smiled. This was the best Hallowe'en Horror Night House ever!

***

Rick was lifted from his reverie by the dislocated voice of the column.

"You must consult the tablet at your side." Rick knew that he did not have such a tablet, but as soon as he extended his right arm to search for it, it was there, on the belt that held his rough hessian robe closed. Beneath the belt he was wearing something akin to a Jedi robe, but which had been dyed a subdued yellow.

He lifted up the tablet, the screen of which showed a small version of the eye of the Realm. As he watched, the eye faded into a map with numerous markers pointing the way to a large tower. Hovering above the tower was an animated cartoon drawing of a beautiful woman with pointed ears protruding through long black hair.

"Save me, Rick." The woman, who looked remarkably like Jennifer Garner, was clearly a grown-up version of Princess Zelda, and she was pleading silently to him.

"Rick," the Eye intoned. "Your mission, should you choose to accept it, is to save the princess. However, if you are captured the realm will disavow you. You are on your own."

Rick waited five seconds for his tablet to explode. It didn't, and so he stepped out of the cave and looked at the colourful world beyond. The shades and hues were so vivid that he could easily have been in Pandora in Disney's Animal Kingdom.

He was halfway up a mountain. Ahead of him lay a valley filled with green pastureland and unusual domesticated animals which might have been sheep if they had four legs and were white. As it was, they were pink and purple and the had hind legs with two short arms. There was a stone hut with a thatched roof at the edge of the pasture, and wisps of smoke curled from its oddly constructed chimney. Rick imagined that the shepherd of these weird creatures might live in that hut and so he planned to head off in that direction.

As soon as it was apparent that he was heading towards the stone building the tablet vibrated. He looked at the screen.

"Good Decision: 300 Points, Choose a Bonus." There appeared before him, suspended in the air, a purple neon outline of a water canteen, a walking staff and a sword. He had only enough points for two items, so he chose the water container and the staff, as he wasn't about to kill anyone. As he reached out the neon items dissolved before his eyes, and he found the real walking staff in his hand and the water carrier hanging at his side.

Rick drank deeply from the water carrier. The water was cold, sweet and pure. It immediately quenched the thirst he had not realised he had been experiencing. As soon as he laid it back by his side it refilled magically.

"I could do with one of these at Universal," he thought to himself.

***

Rick made his way towards the stone cottage; it took a good hour of fast walking over uneven ground, but he felt no fatigue. There was a noise coming from the rear of the cottage. As he approached the back door an older man was standing with his back to Rick. He was sorting fruit. The old man was a jolly round fellow with a goatee beard and two pointy ears either side of a flat cap.

"Welcome Rick, we are so pleased you are here."

The man said all of this without turning around. Rick was surprised but not shocked that the man knew his name. "For there is work to be done and I am too old to do it." The man paused and touched his ears. "My ears have reached the pinnacle of their apex; I have but few days in this realm left to savour. Like all men I fear that I have one more dawn than sunset in my future. That is why the Column of Eslin chose you; your ears are still rounded."

Rick touched his ears automatically; they were still quite rounded, but they now had a distinct point to them. Another man might have been horrified by this slow transition to elfishness, but Rick simply said, "Cool."

The man looked directly at Rick and held up what looked to be the rosiest and most delicious looking apple there had ever been. "Please take a bite." Rick briefly thought of Snow White, but then dismissed the silly idea - after all it was a fairy tale - and took a bite of the fruit. It was delicious to the taste and suddenly his eyes were opened. He saw the princess trapped in a large bedroom in the castle. She was beautiful, for an anime character. She was beckoning him. "Rescue me, Rick!" she was mouthing.

The man said, "If you fall short of energy, or you are feeling dismayed, eat the fruit in your knapsack." Rick was about to say that he had no knapsack when he looked down and saw a cross body bag filled with fruit.

"Do you have any words of wisdom, old man?" Rick asked, possibly politically incorrectly. The man looked at him intensely.

"Follow your quest, travel at quiet times, do not be distracted, avoid lines, watch for the rain - when people will scatter. Remember you will achieve more early in the day and later at night."

All sensible advice, Rick thought as he prepared to set off. Suddenly there appeared in front of him a neon outline of a card. It appeared under a heading of 'bonus'. He reached up and it disappeared.

"Take your leave, use your pass wisely, it will carry you to the front of any crowd."

**

Rick was making his way towards the castle when he came to an abrupt halt. There was standing before him an alien, a monster of sorts. It could have just graduated from the Monster University, if it had not been so stupid. It was, however, also dangerous and big. Very big. It reached out to grab him and squeeze the life from his body.

Rick planted the walking staff into the ground and then swung around it in a move reminiscent of the Kung Fu TV series of his youth. His feet connected hard with the groin of the monster. It folded, groaning; obviously some things do not change across multiple realities. He then clambered onto its back and gripped his hands together across the monster's throat, holding on until it passed out.

The tablet pinged with a new message. "You have defeated the first of the Bindots, purple monsters set to guard the castle which is now a prison." Two new neon choices appeared. This time he took the small sword. Albeit the Brisket Crepe was a real temptation.

The remainder of the day passed travelling, circumnavigating, and occasionally defeating an array of odd-looking beings, until he came across the very human looking 'Torval – The Tempter'.

"Rick, so good to see you at last. I have heard so much about you. I have to admit I am a follower of your work. It's true. A powerful man still needs a hobby for the downtimes when he is not conquering ancient civilisations and stripping them clean of everything that makes them good and wholesome."

The man was as tall as Rick, bald, had pointed ears and an evil look shone in his eye.

"You!" Rick exclaimed, recognising him immediately. "You ruined four of the worlds in my home universe. You took places of magic, animals, the future and movies and exploited them for the money. You had no care for the people who loved those places and who now find them out of their reach."

"Rick." The man laughed. "Those places are cash cows, as is Hyrule. I can make more money for the Realm from less people, it's a win-win," he sneered. "For the rich! Now, join me, forget your quest."

Rick was shocked at the affrontery of the man. He drew his sword. The man withdrew a light sabre and grinned. "Wrong genre, I know. But I have so many universes under my control now, so many marvellous universes."

Rick and the man fought; the sword was more useful against the light sabre than Rick had imagined. "Set down the sword, Rick, you are destined to lose." Rick was inclined to agree until a light appeared at his side. A ghostly figure in a suit and tie appeared. It looked for all the world like Walt Disney. It spoke quietly.

"Rick, you have fought bravely but you cannot overcome Torval today. We can hold him back for a while, but not forever." Rick looked to his left and saw a second suited man with an equally determined look on his face. Roy Disney? He wondered briefly if Michael Eisner was on his way too.

The two spectres swooped on Torval, engulfing him and shouting in accusing tones, "Our legacy". Torval yelled in panic, "Your time has gone, I am the leader now!" Rick took advantage of the confusion, banged his staff on the ground and a portal opened up. He passed through alone. He was at the castle gates. He was exhausted and lay down against the castle walls.

**

Rick awoke after a restful sleep and saw that the sun was rising. He went to the stream to wash. When he saw his reflection, he was shaken. He was becoming more animated by the hour. His face and arms looked as though they had been computer generated, human looking but not quite human. He needed to end this quest and get home before he lost his humanity and was destined to stay and live out his days as an anime character in Hyrule.

He was still pondering how to get past the guards on the gates wearing his strange clothes when a woman appeared. She was young and had long dark hair. Peeking out from her hair were her pointed ears. She was walking from stall to stall examining their merchandise. After a moment she spotted him and walked over.

"I am the Court Emissary and handmaiden to the Princess," she whispered. "We need you to act promptly to save the princess, for today she will be taken to bride by Torval and then all Hyrule will be his to command."

Rick could barely take his eyes off the young woman. She looked like him, especially around the eyes. "Who are you?" he asked.

"My title is Mistress Ney of the Court. Quickly, you need to change into these." She handed him a bag of merchandise that would help him blend in with the crowds entering the castle. She wished him luck and resumed her search for merchandise.

***

Now dressed in the traditional yellow tunic and pantaloons of Hyrule, and wearing a matching hood, Rick joined the crowd. At this rate it would be dusk before he reached the gate. Then he remembered the pass. He summoned it from his bag and found himself at the front of the line. He grinned whilst a woman checked him and his bags for weapons. He passed through, unarmed.

Once inside the walls there appeared in front of him two neon outlines under the title 'special bonus'. One was a large sword; the other was a camera on a stick. He reluctantly chose the sword, even though this would have been the best Vlog ever.

The yellow tunic, crudely hand printed with the Hyrule coat of arms (a shield bearing a magic wand set in front of a rising sun) allowed Rick to pass through the grounds unchallenged. The words beneath the coat of arms must have been in some Latin version of Hyrule as he could not read them. They appeared as:

GhllDeStenvaD ylybe'[2]

Which, to those of us who do not speak Ancient Hyrulish fluently, translates as 'Don't miss the Magic, Don't miss the Sun!'

Rick made his way surreptitiously all the way to the top floor corridor before he met resistance.

***

Pindok the Carrier had once been a large but peaceful man in the land of Annrai. He was always happy to help people carry their loads, which was a good thing for a Demi Giant. He was nine feet tall and heavily bearded. Worst of all, he was reduced to guarding the door to the Princess's bedroom.

"Hagrid?" was Rick's first thought, which was quickly discarded as he took in the enormity of his task. How to take down a giant.

Rick tapped the tablet and the Eye appeared. "You will defeat the giant with cunning, so choose your weapon wisely." There appeared many weapons on the page, as well as many ordinary office and household supplies. It was like a magical Staples store, one that had merged with Dick's Sporting Goods.

---

[2] Actually, we know this is in Klingon before anyone points it out.

Rick chose carefully and set his plan in action.

Rick turned the corner and the Giant stood to attention. He was nine feet of anger and aggression, just waiting to be unleashed. Rick approached him without demur. Then just as the giant was about to strike, Rick pulled out a clipboard and pen and said sternly, "Name?" The giant was not impressed. Rick took the pen and clipboard, clutching them to his chest.

"Who wants to know?" the Giant bellowed.

"I want to know. I am Rick from HR, Hyrule Resources." Rick adopted a harsher tone. "I am the man who decides whether you will be spending the winter in a cosy castle guarding a tiny princess behind a locked door, or knee deep in a swamp controlling the water nymphs!"

The giant was unsettled. He disliked water nymphs. They looked pretty enough but they said spiteful things about his appearance, his personal hygiene and his wits. The also bit you when they were angry.

"Sorry, Master Rick. I am Pindok. What can I do for you?"

"I was sent up to ask why you didn't report at the water wheel in the dungeon at dawn." The giant looked puzzled; Rick continued. "Look, the Antuks blocked the stream overnight and until we clear it, the water wheel will not turn. No wheel turning, no water pumping up the castle for bathing, nor any grinding of grains for breakfast porridge!"

"Could it be a system failure? It has happened before. Those young guys in IT (Inventive Tasks) don't know what they are doing. Most of them are less than a hundred years old," Pindok noted.

"No. We tried turning it off and on again, nothing. We need you to turn the wheel, if you are strong enough."

Pindok raised himself to full height and spoke loudly. "Pindok can turn the Wheel of Time, let alone the castle water wheel." He strode off towards the dungeon where the staff would be as surprised to see him as they would be terrified.

A neon key appeared in front of Rick and as he reached for it, it appeared in his hand. He opened the door. There before him stood the defeated Princess. If there was ever a more beautiful woman, drawn or animated, Rick had yet to see her.

The room was vast and decorated with armour, wall hangings, tapestries and luxurious rugs. There was also a mirror. Rick caught sight of himself. He was almost entirely anime. He now had fully pointed ears and large eyes, with eyebrows that slanted upwards towards the side of his head. The woman spoke in the sensuous and entrancing sing song voice of Jennifer Garner.

"Is it you? Rick of the Garden of Winter. Come to rescue me with his kiss."

This was the kind of challenge that Rick felt he was up to.

"Rick." The beautiful woman was in front of him now, her arms looping his neck. "One kiss from a pure soul like yours and I will be free. Hyrule can be governed with fairness, compassion, inclusivity and diversity. Except the Drockkers and the Pergins, they are just too awful."

"If that's what it takes, I am the hero of this story after all," he replied reluctantly.

"Oh, Rick, we can have lighting without candles, heat without burning wood, paved highways and vehicles powered by the sun. It will be a utopia. There will be restaurants on every corner instead of Walgreens and CVS, because sickness will be banished, and we will have theme parks with no reservations where you can ride without the help of a Genie."

This enchanted woman, who looked destined to spend her life as an eternally thirty-year-old Princess, seemed to have it all worked out. Rick tried his arm.

"Could we have a Mummy Ride in one of the theme parks?" he asked. She smiled.

"Of course, my love." And then her lips met his.

He expected to be swept away with longing, passion and excitement, but all he felt was guilt. Nikki was waiting for him. He needed to return to her. Nikki was the only woman for him. For her part she would never dream of admiring or kissing another man.

The tablet by his side pinged and Rick felt himself drifting away into darkness.

An Outlanderish Story[3]

Nikki awoke in a sitting position. She was in a forest; it was misty and frigid looking, but she felt no chill. This was not a woodland in Florida, it was more akin to a Scandinavian Forest. It was adorned with pines and firs; it was as fragrant as it was beautiful. The mottled sunlight that found its way to the forest floor made the dewy leaves and shrubs sparkle. When she stood, she realised why she felt no chill. She appeared to be wearing an entire wardrobe of clothes at once. Her underwear was a white cotton bodice that tied with string at the waist. Below that were heavy cotton pantaloons and at least two layers of underskirt covered the pantaloons. The tight outer waistcoat that encompassed her upper torso was constructed of a leathery material laced at the front. It too cinched at the waist whilst providing an impressive decolletage. Nikki smiled at that. Over her shoulders she bore a heavy tartan shawl, still warm with her own body heat.

She had never felt so, alluring? She felt like Scarlet O' Hara in Gone with the Wind. However, any similarity to the Antebellum South of the United States was soon dispelled.

"Miss Nicola. The way is safe, you can come with me now." A strong and muscular arm sculpted with roped tendons reached out to her. She was clearly expected to take the hand of this incredibly handsome and rugged Scots warrior, bedecked in traditional dress with a wicked dirk (dagger), hanging from his belt. He pushed his unruly red hair away from his face, revealing opaline eyes that had an iridescent shine to them.

He smiled and Nikki almost fainted. The man with the sensual brogue obviously knew her well and so she followed.

"If we are to find a way through the McDermott lines and back onto Tyrell defended land, we need to move now." The word Tyrell appeared in her

---

[3] Our deepest apologies to Diana Gabaldon. Forgive us.

head spelled as the man had intended, but that man pronounced it very simply, Tirr'l.

The meandering pathway was overgrown and hard to discern but they made good progress. The heroic Clansman led the way and Nikki followed in his wake. She had been cruelly disappointed when the path narrowed to the point where he was obliged to let go of her hand. "I am a married woman, I love Rick," was the mantra she repeated in her head every time her guardian turned to encourage her on, grinning and flashing those eyes, eyes that would have beguiled a saint.

His name was Keithen, she knew that instinctively, just as she knew they were heading to her family stronghold. Castle was not too strong a term for the grey stone fortress that guaranteed security to the Tyrell family. It was, by any standards, a magnificent edifice whose dramatic hallway bore her portrait. The painting was an idealised rendering of Nikki in full clan dress, painted in oils by the famous local artist Jenny McDruitt.

***

Keithen stopped in his tracks and positioned his left arm out horizontally, as if to protect Nikki. They crouched low in the bushes that gave way to the large clearing that was occasionally used for Celtic rituals, and for druid earth magic.

On the right nights of the year fires would be lit and crops, carved icons and figures would be burned. As would the captured arms of the enemy. The earth was magical here and great feats of mystic healing had been celebrated in stories and songs.

"It looks quiet," Nikki whispered, now huddled against Keithan, his musky aroma not at all unpleasant, stimulating her nostrils. He hooked a long arm across her shoulders, sharing his large tartan hunting shawl. Nikki felt warm and secure at the same instant.

"Aye, lass, it's quiet enough. A little too quiet. When the birds and the little forest rascals are staying this quiet, there's usually men about."

It was a long trek around the clearing, but they had no choice. They circumnavigated the ritual ground, keeping low and keeping quiet. Their enemies were not as disciplined. The whisper of a man in the forest carried; it bounced off tree trunks and was strangely unnatural. It also signalled his direction. The best of the Scots hunters used their normal quiet voices which blended more with nature and was less jarring to the trained ear of a soldier, or to the pricked ears of a wary red deer.

They were about to re-join the path that led to the castle just a mile hence, when a voice cried out. They had been spotted. Keithen pushed Nikki in front of him and urged her on. He placed himself between her and the soldiers.

It was the English, more particularly Captain Henry Mullen's troop, that were now in pursuit. Nikki had a history with the man known as 'Scarred Harry'. She had been his hostage until Keithen, and his fellow clansmen freed her in a daring night-time raid, years before.

"Into the burn," Keithen said softly, and they both left the high path and slid down a steep embankment that led to the Craet'th Burn, a dangerous fast flowing stream in the spring, a still pond in the summer, but today it moved laboriously through the autumn forest, thick with debris from the fallen trees. Beavers inhabited the area, damming the stream and forming refreshing bathing pools. The pools remained until the spring snows melted, and the wee burn became a torrent and washed away every obstruction in its hurry to Loch Nairn.

They could hear the confused shouts of their pursuers on the path high above them.

"They're doon in the burn!" shouted one of the Scottish trackers, happy to betray their own for the King's Shilling.

***

Nikki and Keithen crossed and recrossed the burn until they were soaked to the skin. The weather was warm enough, albeit not to Nikki, who appreciated living in Florida, but the slight breeze soon put a chill on your bones when you were drenched.

They were almost clear when Nikki heard the swoosh of an arrow flying close by. She heard a muffled cry from Keithen, followed by the snapping of the arrow. He had presumably been hit but she could not see where from her position ahead of him.

It had been their pursuers last effort as the couple emerged from the woods on defended Tyrell land and soon spotted Le Rêve, a mysterious ring of stones in the forest, where a French speaking *witch* resided.

It was unclear why the French woman had remained behind in the highlands after the departure of her beloved Bonny Prince Charlie.

Pretender to the English throne, Charles had hidden in the moors of Scotland, almost always fractionally ahead of the English government forces. Many Highlanders aided him, and not one of them betrayed him, even for the huge £30,000 reward on offer. Charles was constantly assisted by loyal supporters such as Donald Macleod of Galtrigill, Captain Con O'Neill who took him to Benbecula, and finally the renowned Flora MacDonald, who helped him escape to the Isle of Skye by taking him in a boat disguised as her maid "Betty Burke". Charles evaded capture and left the country aboard the French frigate *L'Heureux*, arriving in France forlorn. But for her own reasons Marie Preese, the witch, remained and served as a healer to the local community.

***

Keithen limped into the old woman's stone shelter. It could not seriously carry the title of house. The old woman laid him on a makeshift table face down. In any event she could not see the arrow until she lifted up Keithen's kilt.

There above strong hirsute legs were a naked pair of the finest male buttocks she had ever seen. Once again, she asked herself why in the highlands the men eschewed underwear.

"Nikki, I want you to yank out what is left of the arrow for me. You are a nurse; you will know what to do." Nikki wanted to say that actually she was a Special Ed teacher at High School, but this did not seem to be the time.

The arrowhead was not buried deep. The thick woollen kilt had done a fine job at absorbing some of the velocity, and it was angled. The sharp pain that accompanied its removal would be painful, but it would pass. A stitch or two would be needed to close the wound. Nikki pulled, the arrow came out cleanly and Keithen only grunted.

The old lady took over, seeing Nikki's hesitation at the sight of blood, and her clear admiration of the man's rear. The old woman stitched the wound before giving Nikki a gourd filled with a strong-smelling ointment.

The woman communicated that it was for Nikki to rub on the ointment to calm the pain and disinfect the man's rear. Nikki did as she was asked and Keithen relaxed as she massaged in the thick balm, muttering under her breath, "I am a married woman. I love Rick.".

***

There was no realistic prospect of Keithen riding a horse for a day or two and they were now a mile or two of rough ground from the castle after their detour.

Marie Preese made guttural sounds in medieval French and drew a map in the dirt. She indicated that just a short distance away stood a shack where they could find transport back to the castle.

They made their way as soon as darkness fell, a full moon lighting their way. Nikki could not help but gaze in wonder at the night sky. Everything was so much sharper and clearer without light pollution from towns and cities.

They soon reached a turf covered shack where a craftsman was fashioning a board from a section of a fallen tree. The carpenter was as strange as the Frenchwoman, but in a mad magician kind of way. He appeared to Nikki to be a Scots madcap version of Doc Brown.

Seeing that Keithen could not sit on a horse comfortably, the carpenter, known as Ronjon the Younger, introduced them to his newest transport for the sick or injured.

The finely carved and highly polished board was as long as a man was tall. It was designed so that one could stand upon it or lay upon it and be pulled along at speed by a horse with a rider. When standing, balance was the great challenge, but after a few spills and wipeouts, Keithen had mastered the board and rode it with his legs splayed and his arms stretched for balance.

Their arrival at the Castle was accompanied by cries of relief, wonder and laughter.

***

Nikki was sitting in front of a roaring fire. Keithen was fast asleep, his head in her lap. She knew that in the morning she would have a choice to make; stay and fight for the Tyrell cause and Bonny Prince Charlie, or return to her own time.

She would worry about that after a good night of rest. For now, she would just take a quick peek to see how Keithen's wound was healing. She was after all a nurse, of sorts.

***

The sun was shining, and the clan were celebrating the eve of All Hallows Day. Some of the younger folk referred to the night-time antics as Mischief Night or Hallowe'en.

Nikki was watching and wondering how to tell Keithen that she must return to her home and own time, when shots rang out. There was artillery too. The woman and children ran for the safe shelter of the castle and the men stood their ground.

This attack was unique. Neither the English nor the opposing fighting clans had dared mount a daylight raid on Tyrell land. Within minutes every man was armed, and they began an ordered retreat of their kinsfolk to the safety of the castle. Keithen and a few others covered the retreat, keeping the English at bay.

Keithen gathered a group of the hardiest fighter around him and, once he had spoken to them, they lined up and charged at a shocked English contingent yelling, "Tyrell for Bonny Prince Charlie." The English scattered.

The ruse worked for a few minutes and then *Scarred Harry* emerged from the trees with two dozen screaming battle hardened soldiers, all armed with muskets. Back in the castle the clansmen were firing down on the English with some success and the attack began to falter. Soon men began to run back towards the cover of the trees, against the orders of Scarred Harry.

Keithen and Nikki were slowly backing towards the castle gates. He had three men fighting against him, but he was like a demon with his sword in one hand and dirk in the other.

Nikki noticed that Scarred Harry had lost his hat and his wig in battle. His demented expression was made all the more terrifying by the terrible scarring of his bald head and an angry weal running across his forehead.

He lifted the musket and smiled. He was aiming at Keithen who was unaware of the danger. Nikki watched as the cock on the musket flew downwards, the flint struck the steel, producing sparks. The steel moved forward, exposing the powder-filled flash-pan to the sparks. There was a brief pause while the powder in the pan ignited, and then the main charge fired, sending the musket-ball on its way.

Keithen heard the shot and turned to see Nikki diving in front of him and covering him with her body. He yelled "Noooo..." but Nikki was already exposed.

Keithen watched, despair creasing his rugged face as the musket ball hit Nikki in the head and she collapsed, possibly dead, to the forest floor.

Back to the Future

Rick and Nikki awoke for a second time. Nikki's head was throbbing to such an extent that she wondered if the musket ball really was responsible. She looked over to see Rick sitting up against a wall, asleep, and making kissing motions with his lips. She woke him up by kicking his legs. He was having too much fun dreaming of kissing, presumably, another woman.

Rick then explained his dream, and when asked who he was kissing he wisely lied that Nikki was the recipient of his lip-based passion. It was an unconvincing lie, but Nikki could forgive him having a crush on a cartoon beauty. Had it been a real woman, it would have been a very different story.

Nikki also felt obliged to explain her dream. "Who was your hunky rescuer?" Rick asked.

"It was you dressed in a kilt," Nikki answered, persuading herself that this white lie would be better for Rick's ego. It turned out that Rick did not even notice the lie, he was busy imagining himself as a Highlander with a large Dirk at his side and another tucked into his gartered socks. "I could never go commando in a kilt, too much opportunity for an incident," Rick shared. Nikki curled her lip at the excess of information.

"Did I say that out loud?" Rick asked.

***

Somehow, during the time that they were dreamily travelling the Scottish Highlands, and the Realm of Zelda, respectively, they had been transported in a panel van to a remote private airport hangar at Orlando International Airport.

As soon as they had consumed the mocktail, and more specifically the gummies, they had passed out. Ingrid Carmody, the witch, and her minder had picked them up and perched them up against the walls of the panel van for the short journey.

The gummies had contained a hallucinogenic drug that Isabel had set in edible gelatin. That drug was variant of LSD, or more properly termed, D-lysergic acid diethylamide. LSD being a manmade chemical genetically reconstructed from ergot, a fungus that grows on certain grains. Probably the most powerful hallucinogen available, it changes the way reality is perceived, and alters moods accordingly. It had certainly worked on Rick and Nikki.

The van had been parked inside the empty rented marquee, out of sight of everyone, and most certainly out of sight of Universal Security.

The marquee also had the advantage of being at the very edge of the property and so after a minute and passing through an automatic gate, they were on the highway.

***

Ingrid Carmody in her guise as the witch, had drugged them sufficiently to transport them on her private jet to the family's summer ranch in Arizona, where they would be made to pay for the unjust imprisonment of her beautiful fiancé, Carswell Judd.

Meanwhile back at Universal Studios the Lords, who had accompanied the twosome to the park, but who parted outside the special event location, became worried. It was pushing 2pm and they had been expecting Rick and Nikki back within the hour. Furthermore, neither of them were responding to their telephones.

Knowing that she was probably over-reacting, Lucy Lord sent out a message on Rix Flix to see if there were other followers of the couple in the park, and who may be prepared to help in a search. Six people responded in minutes.

They elicited the help of these other Flixters in the park and began a grid search for Nikki and Rick. He should be easy to find with his height and wearing a yellow tee shirt.

Executive Producers Jeremy and Kim Smith were tasked with finding out if the couple were still in the preview area. However, when Jeremy and Kim arrived, there was no sign of a preview or private event. The signage had gone. There only remained a plastic barrier. Kim was not one for giving up so easily and so when no-one was watching she pulled Jeremy behind her and up the plant obscured path that led to the marquee.

They were concerned to discover that this supposed private event appeared to be non-existent. Kim pushed the door, expecting it to be locked, but it wasn't. Jeremy led the way. Inside hung heavy black curtains. To one side was a movie poster.

They pushed their way through the curtains expecting to see a haunted house. There was nothing at all. It was just an empty marquee. Rick and Nikki had disappeared.

The Searchers

The Universal Security Team were reluctant to become involved in a search for two adults who could easily have left the park under their own auspices, for a medical emergency for example. However, they explained that if the couple had not showed by 5pm they would check at the exits as day visitors left the park, and then they would check the HHN waiting areas, but that was the best that they could do for non-family members reporting an unknown incident.

Not prepared to give up in such suspicious circumstances, the Lords and The Smiths met with two more couples at Chez Alcatraz and told their story to Murph, the barman. Murph was concerned too. He called a friend in security and explained the problem. Minutes later he had a call back.

He was told that a panel van had been seen leaving the vicinity of the marquee, but he was also informed that there were no cameras recording vehicle tags/number plates. Security also suggested that the actual private preview may well have been at a venue off site, and so the departure of the panel van may have an entirely innocent explanation.

"If Disney can send Interstellar hotel guests to a space hotel in a converted U-Haul Van and charge them six thousand dollars for the privilege, who knows what is now *de rigueur* in theme park trends," the security manager joked somewhat inappropriately.

No-one was convinced. Especially Murph. He spoke quietly as he handed over the reins to the other bartenders.

"I think the time has come to speak to *Crazy Colin* at the back gate."

***

Colin Wright was originally recruited to Universal gate security in the mid 1980's when this was still a building site. He was mainly tasked with keeping rubberneckers away. Then when the park opened, Universal applied for a permit to have a permanent security booth at the gate. The simple single space building application was granted but Colin somehow bullied the builders into constructing the booth so that it had a separate tiny second space, this one containing the mini kitchen, a stand for a TV and (late one night when no-one was around) his recliner. With a/c provided by Universal, it was Colin's tiny home from home.

The booth had actually become redundant in 1998 when the backlot entry system went electronic, but nobody in HR had the nerve to sack Colin. So, he stayed until he was 65. Then they paid him off with a generous Universal Pension, which replaced his meagre salary. Colin loved the leaving party, adored the cake and he treasured the gold watch. But on Monday morning, to everyone's dismay he was back in his booth at 6am prompt. There he stayed during the pandemic, doing a sterling job writing down every license tag, in and out, on his trusty clipboard. Filing data that no-one would ever see. Until today.

***

Rick and Nikki found themselves sitting side by side on a corporate jet. Their seats were as comfortable as Lazy Boys, but as well as lap belts they were secured to the seat arms with zip ties, and they had been warned that this situation would likely persist during the flight.

"Typical," Rick whispered to his worried wife. "First time on a corporate jet and we don't get to enjoy the food, or champagne." Nikki shook her head. Every now and again her husband's priorities concerned her.

Ingrid Carmody took a seat opposite them. "Well, we have four and a half hours flying time to get to know one another." The plane began to taxi, and she fastened her seat belt. "Once we are in the air, I will release the zip ties, so long as you promise not to endanger the aircraft."

Everyone braced themselves for take-off, which happened a lot quicker than on a commercial jet. Nikki looked at their kidnapper and tried to unravel her motives. The woman was rich, superbly groomed and quite attractive. Her facial features were arranged a little unusually and so she would never be a classical beauty, but who was?

"If you behave, I see no reason why we shouldn't have a little 'in flight' champagne, and the galley is usually stocked with gourmet food, albeit my particular favourite is my personal chef's take on the In'n'Out Burger and fries. I usually ensure that we have a couple of fresh Double-Doubles on board."

Ingrid Carmody smiled pleasantly. Nikki looked across at Rick. He was smiling too, but at the thought of the burgers. He had missed lunch, after all.

* * *

Murph set down his phone after speaking to Crazy Colin and reported back to the gathered Flixters, who were anxious for news.

"OK. He has the tag number of the panel van. It's the only van that left the park in the time slot." He paused whilst he located a number on his mobile phone. "There isn't anything else you can do here. Try to enjoy yourselves and check in with me at end of shift, around 1am. I am calling a friend at Orlando Police. It's time our tax dollars were set to work!"

The Flixters dispersed, but Lucy Lord, her husband, Adam and the Smiths agreed to meet up for dinner at Finnegans later to discuss what else they could do, if anything.

Murph rang the Orlando Police and asked to be patched through to Officer Ray Dalton. Initially the heavily Irish accented despatcher refused to put Murph through. "Is that Deidra?" he asked. "Yes," she answered somewhat quizzically. "This is Murph at Chez Alcatraz. You and I did the voice over for the St Patrick's day ad during lockdown." He did not add 'before you were furloughed and had to find a new job with the Police'. After minimal pleasantries Deidra softened and put Murph through on the grounds that it was an emergency.

Murph had encountered the police officer earlier in the year when a serial killer was targeting Rick and Nikki. The entire event had been recounted by the author J Jackson Bentley in the book "Zero Days Without Incident". It was a supposedly fictional account of events, but Murph and Officer Dalton knew the truth.

***

Ray Dalton listened carefully and then told Murph he would have to call him back. The panel van's vehicle tags were run, and it was discovered that the hire van had passed through several tolls and was clearly on its way to the airport. Dalton ran down the corridor and directly into the Chief's office. The door was continually open these days as per the new 'Openness' operational policy.

"Chief, I have reason to believe that the RixFlix vloggers, Rick and Nikki have been kidnapped."

The man behind the desk dropped his head into his hands. "Not again," he said sorrowfully.

"Dalton, you are friendly with them, can't you persuade them to move to California? They have theme parks, and lots of empty houses. Especially since the Californians started coming here in droves." He paused whilst he looked his officer directly in the eye.

"For heaven's sake, Ray, this is the third time this year and its only September! First it was the serial killer, then that crazy robbery and car chase, now it's a Hallowe'en Hijack! What have they got planned for the Holidays? Heaven save us from amateur sleuths!"

Despite his deep misgivings, the Police Chief considered running an amber alert, but there was a fear that this would alarm the kidnappers, if there were any, and so they tracked the van by CCTV. They lost track of it at Heintzelman Boulevard.

"They are at the private airfield at McCoy Airport Eastside. The kidnappers must be smuggling them out on a private plane," Officer Dalton shouted across the room to Gemma, who was co-ordinating.

"OK, Ray. Leave it to me I'll have the airport police there in five minutes."

The police did indeed arrive at the Eastside hangar, within the promised five minutes, but the van and the plane had gone. The plane was on its way across the gulf when the Police Chief was patched through to the pilot.

"Sorry Chief Palmer, I can't help you. We are flying to California with Ms Ingrid Carmody of Dionsus Biotech as our only passenger. I think you may have been misled."

The chief did not give up and insisted on speaking to Ingrid personally. She was politeness and charm itself. She chuckled at the idea that a multinational biotech company would kidnap a couple of theme park vloggers.

"What on earth would be our motive?"

The chief wondered the exact same thing and thanked her for her assistance. When he cut off the speakerphone he spoke to Gemma and to Officer Dalton.

"She was too slick for my liking. Have her plane met at the LAX Private Terminal when it lands this evening, by real Police, the LAPD, not the airport police, understood?" They nodded.

Room for Escape

Gavin Collison had been the Manager out at the Carmody Ranch, in Flagstaff, Arizona for over a decade. To be honest he would have taken any job just to be close to Ingrid. He was smitten and always had been.

The ranch was less than a mile, as the crow flies, from Flagstaff Pulliam Airport runway. It had once belonged to a famous movie actor, known for his macho cowboy roles and his iconic eye patch. The ranch had never made any profit, but it was a peaceful place to ride and rest, away from the hustle and bustle of the world, and for rich people it was a good tax write-off.

The Flagstaff Pulliam Airport enjoyed an open aspect some 5 miles south of Flagstaff, in Coconino County, Arizona. The airport was friendly and as well as private flights it was serviced by carriers American Eagle and United Express. It was also used for general aviation, like flying lessons and had even appeared in a couple of well-known movies.

The pilot of the Dionsus Biotech Bombardier Challenger 350 aircraft had waited until he was over Texas before notifying a change of destination. Air traffic logged the change without demur or indeed any real thought. The rich often made their decisions based on a whim. Who were the flight monitors to intervene or complain?

The plane touched down at 4pm Mountain Standard time, 6pm Eastern, and taxied to a private hangar. Neither Rick nor Nikki were in the mood for fighting against burly armed men and so they complied with instructions and found themselves sitting in a luxurious Lincoln Navigator, fine white leather everywhere.

A little lightheaded from the champagne and stomachs filled with the best burgers they had ever encountered, they watched as the barren landscape passed by the blacked-out windows.

They were worried. Their daughters had no idea where they were and their friends in the park must be frantic, but when they saw the friendly, open face of Gavin Collinson, they relaxed.

"Howdy," he said, tugging at the brim of his Stetson. "Y'all must be tired, let me show you to your suite."

Rick was the first to speak when they were left alone in the suite. It had the floor area of most houses. "Nikki, this has to be the most luxurious kidnapping in the history of kidnappings. What is going on here? Is she some mad fan?"

"I don't think so, Rick," Nikki replied as she lifted up a custom-made track suit with her name tastefully embroidered on the left side of the chest. "I have an idea that this will be the most expensive garment I have ever worn." It was designer stylish, comfortable and so soft to the touch it had to be silk chenille.

Ingrid Carmody appeared at the door. "Please, shower, freshen up and dress in the clothes provided. You will be completing the first of two escape rooms this evening when it is dark." She looked down at her watch. "Let's say three hours' time."

The couple flopped onto the amazing bed that might have been made for them. The bed was so large that they could comfortably each take a side and still fit a family of four between them.

They rolled together and Rick encompassed Nikki in his arms. Her head rested on his chest; her hair still smelled of her favoured coconut shampoo.

"Don't worry Nikki. I'll think of something."

***

Ingrid ushered the track suited couple into the first escape room. It was themed on Back to the Future.

"You will be locked in Doc Brown's office. You need to escape into room two where you will find a DeLorean. The DeLorean is the key to your escape."

The door closed and locked behind them and they moved into an office that might have been hi tech in 1985 but which now looked dated. They looked around for clues as to how to open the cage that would allow them to open the exit door and escape.

After a few minutes of looking around Nikki noticed a picture of a dog on the wall. It was more than a photo, it was an electronic photo frame of sorts. The dog was looking sadly at them and under the picture was a label or cartouche, which was empty. Nikki had an idea. She touched the empty cartouche and a flashing cursor appeared. Seeing that the dog was a Labrador liker her own, she typed, Einstein. The photo changed and the dog was happy. A panel below the picture popped open and there was a plastic card inside. It read:

"Biff Tannen, Auto Detailing." On the rear there was a challenge. "Meet me in the future, Butthead, if you are quick."

The couple searched the office high and low for almost thirty minutes before Rick looked at a licence tag screwed to the wall.

"Nikki, if we are quick we won't be…." he read off the plate "Outtatime".

Rick tried to dislodge the tin California plate, but it wasn't moving. He scratched his head. Nikki tried and noticed that it moved sideways a fraction. She pushed and slid. The plate moved to reveal a wall safe. There was no keypad or keyhole, just a blank panel.

Rick moved quickly and placed the card flat against the panel. The safe door clicked and opened. The key to the cage was inside. Within a minute they were out of the cage and into a room that looked like a garage with a roller shutter door, but most importantly, there stood a DeLorean time machine.

***

After dinner the Lord's and the Smiths met up with Murph. Officer Ray Dalton was on the speakerphone.

"They never made it to LAX, they were diverted to Flagstaff, albeit we had to threaten a federal warrant to get even that information. The plane touched down almost four hours ago.

We don't know for sure where they went after landing but I have a message here from the FBI who have informed us that the DoJ database in Virginia includes information that Ingrid Carmody, the woman who spoke to the chief from the plane, owns a company that run a ranch nearby. She is a person of interest because she has acquired special clearance to visit a federal facility. They are not sure why she needs to visit the facility; it wasn't explained on the sheet. But you probably know that Pharma companies pay inmates to participate in medical trials.

Anyway, the chief is calling the Flagstaff PD as we speak. I'll call back."

"Everyone, follow me, and try to avoid the crazies out there. We have no time to waste," Murph said.

The five set off in the direction of the backlot behind Pantages but in so doing had to navigate their way through crowds, scare actors and scare zones, all carefully placed to shock and terrify visitors. HHN was great again this year.

They pushed their way through the crowds until they were off set. They were now in a quiet backstage area. Murph led them through an area where zombies were stripping off bloodied clothing, prosthetics and make-up. These actors were done for the night.

Murph sat down at a canteen style table and unfolded his laptop. It booted up immediately, as it was new. With the dexterity and speed of a hacker he scoured the web, the good and the bad, looking for something, anything that would help.

The others stood around feeling useless but revelling in the fact that they were backstage at Universal.

"Here, this might be useful. I scoured the delivery companies DHL, UPS and the others to see if they delivered anything to the ranch that might give us a reason to send in the police.

Interestingly, on the logisticsarizona.com website you can track your deliveries. They also give you a two-week historical overview of deliveries and attempted deliveries, if you type in your address.

I typed in the ranch address and found that FedEx delivered four consignments to the farm in the last two weeks. Each one was a full load itself, that is each one was a truckload."

"That's a lot of deliveries," Lucy Lord noted. Her husband Adam wondered, silently, how many truckloads a normal ranch had delivered by FedEx in any given year. Murph typed away at the keyboard and said:

"This series of deliveries was earmarked for:

Iris Coulthard, EscapetoEntertainment Inc.

IC, an alias for Ingrid Carmody perhaps, and *EtoE* is the name of the company who rented the marquee." He stopped speaking as he continued typing. "Well, well, well." The group stared at Murph, who was leaning back in his chair.

"It seems that the delivery to Flagstaff was sent from the very same Californian company that is supplying Universal Orlando with everything they need for the new escape rooms on CityWalk.

Maybe our intrepid friends are getting their free preview after all."

***

Gavin Collison was clearing out the Lincoln Navigator for detailing when he came across a metal box around six inches wide, nine inches long and three inches deep under the front passenger seat. It was stamped with the letters RFID. He was puzzled but he took it inside and set it down on his workbench.

Having cleared the vehicle for the valet clean, Gavin opened the box on his workbench. It was latched but it wasn't locked. He withdrew two mobile phones and a camera on a stick.

He laid them on the bench and switched them on. They came to life but each of the phones demanded a password to get beyond the lock screen. He tried the obvious codes, 0000, 1111, 1234, as well as a few others but the phones resisted.

"Boss. Mystic Girl is playing up. Can you take a look." That Arabian mare had been a nightmare since returning from racing in Virginia in the spring. Gavin left everything where it was and walked quickly to the stable.

***

Ray Dalton absorbed the information that Murph had emailed to him. It was good intelligence, but it still did not place Rick or Nikki at the scene in Flagstaff, neither did it indicate that they were in any danger and so it wasn't enough for a warrant. He was beside himself with worry.

Why would you take somebody, deny that you had them with you, and then divert to a remote ranch at the last minute, unless you meant them harm? You wouldn't. Ray was becoming worried that this would be the couple's last ever HHN. His depressive train of thought was broken.

"Ray, over here, quickly." Ray ran over to Officer Jane Karowski. "Ray, someone has switched on both phones. They have been out of signal for hours, but they have just pinged.

They are in Flagstaff, just south of the airport."

Back at the Carmody Ranch Gavin returned to his workbench, having settled the horse, and gave up on trying to decode the phones. He switched them off and placed them back in the RFID box, cosing the lid.

But unknown to him it was too late. The phones had been pinged, a signal had been sent and received.

***

Rick and Nikki had fulfilled most of the requirements for opening the car, but they were now stuck. The replica car could only be opened with a remote key fob, and they did not know where it was.

"If you want to go for a ride, try a re-run." Rick read out the clue for the fiftieth time. What did that mean? "A re-run of what?"

Nikki leapt up from the bench and crossed to the 1950's TV which was switched off. There was a radial switch to turn it on and another to tune it in. She turned the first knob and the TV sprung to life, but it was just showing noise. She turned the second knob to channel number 2 and Jackie Gleason appeared on the screen as Ralph, who was dressed as a spaceman.

"Rick, this is a re-run. Marty told the Baines family that he had seen this episode as a rerun." Rick stood up and crossed the room as Nikki tried to figure out how this helped them, as surely it must.

Nikki pulled at the knob, and it slid out in her hand. Attached to the end that had been inside the TV set was a black plastic key fob. She squeezed it and the gull wing doors to the DeLorean began to rise.

They both cried with joy as they took their seats in the car and closed the doors. Rick turned the key that had been left in the ignition and every light in the cabin came to life.

Rick took a moment to take it all in and then turned the gear shift ninety degrees and switched on the time circuits. Suddenly all of the lights in the room went out. A second later the scene presented in front of them was Hill Valley 1955. They were parked beside a Bluebell Motel billboard.

"When this baby hist 88 miles per hour you are going to see some serious…." Rick wasn't allowed to finish his sentence.

"Yes, we know, just put your foot down and get us out of here!" Nikki commanded.

As soon as the simulator had them accelerating, the screen changed, and they appeared to be screaming through Hill Valley towards the courthouse. They reached 88mph just as they reached the courthouse. Suddenly the whole room was filled with steam, and they could see nothing. When the steam cleared the roller shutter door had gone and they were faced with a room depicting Hill Valley Town Square circa 1985.

"Well done….. you have escaped!" Neon words flashed up on a screen above their heads as they exited the DeLorean.

Rick and Nikki walked into the lounge where food and drink was laid out, along with a tee shirt for each of them reading:

"I escaped Back to the Future."

We only have five minutes left; somebody has to die!

"I find it hard to believe that Gavin Collison would have anything to do with kidnapping," Sheriff John Duluth pointed out to the deputy who had just come off the phone to Orlando Police. "Gavin is one of the nicest guys we ever have to deal with in these backwoods." The deputy agreed without speaking.

"However, we can't ignore a viable threat to life reported by another police department. So, take a ride out to the ranch and see if they can explain how the phones of these two missing Floridians have been pinged at their cell tower.

But be careful. The Carmodys are major financial contributors to this community."

***

Rick and Nikki were exhausted, but Ingrid Carmody was annoyed that they had beaten her Back to the Future escape room with such ease, and so she was now introducing them to her second, and most diabolical locked room, an escape based on Jurassic Park. She grinned as she gave them a final briefing.

"Please do not be cavalier, these animatronic dinosaurs will bite, and the smaller critters might just have some of my famous venom in their fangs and claws. Best of luck."

As soon as she finished speaking the wall ahead of Rick and Nikki lifted and they felt the warm humid, and somewhat fetid air overwhelm them. They were standing in a prehistoric jungle.

Very quickly both Rick and Nikki were scratched and bruised. It seemed to be all but impossible to remove the artefacts and clues without being mauled.

Despite the harshness of the challenges, they eventually managed to progress to the third room, a kitchen set, based on the first film. Somewhere in this stainless-steel utopia was the clue that would see them safely into the final room when the last task awaited, but where was it?

***

It was close to midnight in Orlando and the Flixters were worn out. They had spent the night queuing for the ten available houses, avoiding scare actors at five scare zones, and trying to find a seat in one of the two shows.

Notwithstanding all of the fun, they were still worried about Rick and Nikki. Murph had circulated an email that told them the local Flagstaff Sherriff would be paying a visit to the Carmody Ranch, looking for their friends. A visit which should have taken place by now. After all, it was almost 10pm in Flagstaff and the sleepy mid-western town was probably closing up for the night, at least in their imagination.

***

Rick and Nikki were crouched down beside a food preparation unit, hiding from a potential predator. A raptor was on their scent. The couple had come to the conclusion that no matter what they were able to achieve within these walls, Ingrid Carmody had no intention of letting them live.

Rick was as angry as Nikki had ever seen him. He was going to go down fighting. He would not slip silently into the long goodnight. As the shadow of the raptor passed over them, Rick grabbed the only weapon within reach, a large stainless-steel ladle. He was going into battle with the world's most dangerous predator armed with kitchenware.

As he grabbed the ladle something unexpected happened. The rack holding the ladle turned ninety degrees and a stainless-steel food preparation surface area slid out from behind it.

The two vloggers immediately recognised the potential importance of the trick ladle and stood up.

There on the newly exposed surface were a series of rough drawings. They looked like a selection of pictures from the original Jurassic Park story board. They both saw these as a clue and examined each panel carefully.

"How could we have missed it, Rick?" Nikki yelled excitedly. She pointed at a single drawn panel; it showed a hand holding a can of shaving cream.

Two minutes later they spotted a can of Barbasol shaving cream on a high shelf. Rick stretched up and lifted it down. Nikki quickly unscrewed the bottom of the can. There, concealed in the can was not a dinosaur DNA sample, but a key.

The couple split up and looked for a concealed keyhole. Rick shouted across to Nikki. He was standing in front of what looked like a walk-in freezer. It was locked but the handle had a keyhole.

The couple held hands and kissed passionately before they opened the door that completed their escape. They needed to be prepared for what awaited them on the other side.

***

Gavin Collinson was certain that the deputy's description of the visiting couple having been abducted was way off base. Ingrid had always been eccentric, but she wouldn't hurt anyone. Surely?

He showed Deputy Koontz the RFID lockbox, complete with the phones and then led him to the state-of-the-art sectional building that housed the experimental entertainment studio. Ingrid would explain everything. The original large concrete pad had once housed a stable block that doubled as a sound stage when its original owner was too ill to shoot on a Hollywood Sound Stage.

***

Ingrid Carmody howled in frustration when the CCTV showed a couple of hicks from Florida defeat her impossible escape rooms. In her arrogance it never crossed her mind that this couple had foiled a serial killer and rescued an ancient artefact by anything other than dumb luck. But really, did anyone ever have that much luck.

She grabbed her father's old handgun. It was a Desert Eagle 44 Magnum; it was far too large for her but at this distance it was going to inflict a fatal injury wherever it hit.

The escape room door opened and out stepped Rick and Nikki. They did not seem to be surprised to be confronted with a gun. Rick stepped in front of Nikki. He would take the bullet and hope that he could disable the woman before she could take aim at Nikki. The truth was that a 44 Magnum round would probably pass straight through him.

In that moment Rick accepted his fate and in fractions of a second, he saw Nikki in her high school flag uniform, then laughing as they shared their first meal together and their eyes met over a pizza. He remembered holding her hand as she gripped it tightly at the film of People Under the Stairs.

He recalled how they were both tearful at the announcement of their first pregnancy and so joyful at the births.

Ingrid raised and pointed the gun. Rick spoke calmly.

"You can go ahead and shoot but you will never have what we have shared, never. I pity you."

Ingrid was shaken. Inside she knew that her love for Carswell Lawrence Judd would never be reciprocated. She had known love, dedication and loyalty well beyond the norm, but she had rejected Gavin far too many times for him to risk trying again.

She was about to pull the trigger when the external door opened behind her.

***

Gavin was stunned when he saw Ingrid pointing her dad's gun. The Deputy reacted immediately and unclipped his own weapon, all too late. Ingrid spun around and instinctively fired at the Deputy.

Gavin could see what was about to happen and moved towards Ingrid. The powerful ordnance flew from the barrel and destroyed the single heart that had been dedicated to her since sixth grade.

As Gavin Collison fell, the deputy demanded that she drop the gun. He had no need. Ingrid discarded the gun voluntarily. Sobbing, she fell to her knees, cradling the head of the rapidly failing foreman.

"Gavin, you can't die. I'm so sorry." She kissed his forehead.

Rick and Nikki watched in horror as Gavin Collision proved himself to be worthy of the love of any woman. The light in his eyes was dimming but he was still able to speak.

"Ingrid, I forgive you. It wasn't your fault. I only ever loved once. It was you." He struggled for breath as he began to pass over. "It was always you."

Ingrid Carmody would not let go of Gavin's body until the paramedics sedated her fifteen minutes later.

HHN 31: Don't Go Alone

By the time Rick and Nikki attended the last night of HHN 31 to make a livestream, Ingrid Carmody was in a secure facility. She would never recover from the complete mental collapse she had suffered.

Her brother had visited Carswell Lawrence Judd in Federal Prison and informed him that there would be no appeals, no funding for prison luxuries. In fact, Dillon Carmody made it clear he would use his wealth to make Judd's life a misery for the remainder of his days.

The Mummy Returns had indeed returned and the first Citywalk Escape room would soon be opened. Perhaps the beloved title couple would give them a miss. Perhaps their daughter Courtney could take care of those videos with her friends.

Murph, on a rare night off, celebrated the last night of HHN with a dinner at Toothsome's on Citywalk. Alongside the special guests, Rick and Nikki, were the Lords and the Smiths, as well as Officer Dalton. Even the Police Chief had been persuaded to attend. He had some great brochures about property in Palo Alto, California in his pocket. If Rick and Nikki weren't moving, then he was seriously considering it.

There was a toast made that all would enjoy a happy, carefree and festive season. It was sincerely meant but everyone worried that it was a pipedream.

Across Orlando in Lake Nona a man was producing a poster and flyer for the first ever Theme Park Vlogging Awards, to be presented on Christmas Week 2022. A YouTube special would cover the black-tie event.

On the list of nominees were Taylor Strickland, the Trackers, PC Dev, Mammoth Club, RixFlix and many, many others. It sounded like a great event and a wonderful idea.

And it would have been, if celebrating the season by making awards, and not murder, had been his prime objective.

Original Cover Art

J JACKSON BENTLEY

A RixFlix Holiday Murder Mystery

Murder at the Raven's Claw

fidus

J JACKSON BENTLEY

Murder at the Raven's Claw

A RixFlix Holiday Special Short Story

Edited by Susan Whitfield, Vice President, RixFlix

Published by Fidus USA
An imprint of www.FidusPress.com
All rights reserved. Copyright J Jackson Bentley 2022

This is a work of fiction. Real world places, people, characters, and companies are re-imagined and used in a fictitious setting throughout. No similarity to any actual real-life characteristics, actions or behaviours is intended.

It's the Holidays; Rick and Nikki have been nominated in the Inaugural Vlogger Awards. The awards venue is a mysterious remote country, house and they have not read much Agatha Christie. Murder Ahoy! The Raven is the representative emblem of Ravenclaw.

Preface
December 2022

Chuck Benson adopted his 'American' name in the dark days when having a Latin name was considered a disadvantage in the media, but that was decades ago. Nonetheless, only his mother called him Xavier these days.

Suave and handsome with impossibly black hair, Chuck smiled a fifty-thousand-dollar smile that dazzled the camaras. His complete mouth restoration with titanium implants would have been a luxury for most people but for a Fox local news anchor and local personality it was money in the bank.

"Chuck, can you host a Theme Park Vlogger awards dinner at Lake Nona, second week of December?" the young intern's voice carried across the make-up room as Chuck was having his foundation applied. He was approaching sixty now and he badly needed to look forty.

"No way, Milly. I am still recovering from hosting the Grouting Contractors Awards dinner. It was hard work; do you know there are no jokes about grout worthy of the name?"

The make-up lady chipped in.

"I have one." She paused while Chuck grimaced and then she shared her joke. "Did you know that after achieving universal peace, the Guardians of the Galaxy settled down and opened a floor tile business. Apparently, they called it *I am Grout!*"

Chuck would have shaken his head in disapproval if he was allowed to move. "Tell them I am fully booked for December," he responded.

"OK, but they are offering two thousand dollars for four hours of your time," Milly the intern said quietly as she turned to leave, knowing that her boss would have second thoughts.

"Clear my diary and search the internet for jokes about whatever the awards are for, Vlogging or whatever they call it now," the aging presenter shouted after her.

"Will do," Milly replied, smiling. As she departed, she grinned widely at the make-up lady and asked: "Do you know why tilers won't take a day off?" The make-up lady dutifully shook her head. "They are afraid of missing grout."

Chuck Benson sighed. Why couldn't he ever remember jokes?

***

Across Orlando, close to Lake Nona in a remote but large historic house in the forest just off Cromwell Road, a man was producing a poster and flyer for the first ever *Theme Park Vlogging Awards*, to be presented at Christmastime 2022. A YouTube special livestream would cover the premiere of the black-tie event.

On the list of nominees were Taylor Strickland, the Trackers, PC Dev, Mammoth Club, RixFlix and many, many others. It sounded like a great event and a wonderful idea.

And it would have been, if celebrating the season by giving awards had been the man's prime objective.

***

At the same time the flyers and poster were being designed, theme park vloggers from all around Orlando, in California and in New York were busy confirming their 'Handles' on You Tube. These were the names that they would be using on their channels in the future, and for most of them they were the names they had been using for years. At least now these 'handles' were protected on YouTube and usurpers could not piggyback on the popularity of established creators.

Soon the top twelve nominated vloggers would be invited to attend the awards dinner at the aptly named historic Guest House 'The Raven's Claw'.

Most would recognise the name as one of the houses at Hogwarts School of Witchcraft and Wizardry, but none would research its history or eccentric owner.

Perhaps if they had they would have turned down the invitation and been sure to survive long enough to welcome in 2023.

Part One: Recent History

1

Menlo Park, California. USA, Summer 2006.

Harrison Keeps was smiling. He had been smiling for an entire week now, even when he was asleep. Harry was living the dream; **YouTube** had launched a year ago and his channel *Theme Park Life* was finding an audience hungry for vicarious sunshine, Disney, Universal and fun.

Living in Orlando and being the proud owner of the first compact camera specifically designed for video blogging; Vlogging was what the Californians had chosen to call it. He was ideally placed to report on the daily activities at the major parks close to his Central Florida home.

He could produce high quality videos thanks to a Canon Camera that allowed him to shoot video in HD and which could carry a miniature shotgun microphone that produced half decent sound. His early attempts at video editing were fine, but the resulting videos really needed more polish, and luckily the fledgeling YouTube was anxious to help.

Harrison listened as Wendy Dennis and Ralph Kemp from YT Creator Services explained what they could do for him. Ralph was speaking and Wendy was smiling widely in support.

"Harry, YouTube has taken off big style since last year, but we are weighed down with commercially produced videos that have been professionally edited, often as a platform to sell music. At the other end of the scale, we have poorly produced content showing amateur videos that bounce around so much the viewer gets motion sickness.

We at YT Creator Services, are aiming for the middle ground, the content provider who takes pride in their work but who is independent and free to make their own decisions. In short, people like you.

If you will allow us, we would like to take your raw videos, give them to one of our video whizz kids, let them add royalty free music, and release them onto your channel on Mondays and Fridays.

It will be your work; you will always have editorial control, but we will tidy it up and guarantee you a thousand views a day. How does that sound?"

Harrison signed on the dotted line an hour later. As far as online video content was concerned it was the Wild West out there, but he was happy to be there at its birth, if not its conception.

***

By the autumn and back at home in Central Florida, each of Harrison's posts had 100,000 regular viewers. He had double that number in subscribers. There was a genuine demand for his theme park videos, ride videos and updates. YouTube paid Harrison a small commission and offered their editing services free, for a limited time. They were determined to open up the video marketplace to Middle America, and what better way than to have people live out their dreams of the vacation of a lifetime on their website. Perhaps even more importantly, Middle America was also where the advertisers were now targeting their spending.

His Nokia E50 cell phone was small, sleek and blessed with a colour screen above the keyboard. It also had the option of changing ringtones. A tinny rendition of Ghostbusters rang out; it was his favourite film and favourite Universal Studios ride.

"Harrison Keeps cell phone," he answered, ensuring that everyone knew he had a mobile phone of his own. It was a Disney Media representative. She was offering him another weekend at Disney, this time in the Contemporary North Resort, which had just been fully refurbished. In return for his free VIP stay and food, he was expected to write a blog and submit a video to YouTube.

"I'll do my best, but I'm busy at present. Universal are accommodating me on site at a Premium Hotel to attend the premiere of a new ride."

Harrison knew he would eventually take up Disney's offer, but why make it easy for them? When he was told that a limo service would pick him up at his house on Friday, the deal was done.

Life was great, he was living the dream, most of all he could now leave his job as a cost controller for an aerospace company and still have enough to live on.

2

Carshalton Securities, Downtown Orlando, 2008.

The country's economy was in deep trouble. Subprime mortgage lending was to blame, whatever that was. But that didn't worry Harrison, he had made $720,000 dollars in the last two years alone with advertising and royalties.

He had used half the money to buy a thirty-year lease on a foreclosed, fully furnished historic home by Lake Nona with thirteen bedrooms and seven bathrooms. He had paid cash. No mortgage for him. Albeit it had just about cleared out his checking account.

The house itself had been exquisitely furnished in period style by the old lady who died recently in the master bedroom, probably of loneliness. It was a big place, and she wasn't very mobile.

Harrison would wander from room to room to remind himself of what he owned, him being the son of a single mother and a college dropout. He especially loved the ballroom with its wood panelled walls and hardwood dancefloor. That room alone was thirty feet wide and sixty feet long.

He knew that he would now have to work harder to retain his place in the top ten of Vloggers. YouTube had become more corporate. Gone were the friendly calls and offers of help. He was on his own, apart from his part time editor and graphics guru, Jennie.

New, younger people were encroaching on his space, young pretty girls were flashing their white teeth and leading male viewers on with their endless enthusiasm and physical appeal. Men with exotic moustaches, slicked back hair and magnetic personalities were broadcasting daily.

But Harry had a plan and he had invested his money wisely. His great plan would be sure to rock the vloggersphere. The young mavericks would have to take a back seat and watch. They didn't have the resources to match his grandiose plans.

***

Harry had been waiting in the lobby for some time. He had never been kept waiting by his friend and financial advisor before. He first started to worry when in the space of ten minutes, half a dozen Carshalton Securities employees crossed the lobby, each one crying, each one carrying a box.

"You can go up now, Mr Keeps," an unfamiliar agency receptionist announced.

***

Darius Carshalton had lived in the shadow of his father for too long, and so when the chance arose to make the company, and himself, a quick fortune he bought subprime mortgage packages by the hundred, diverting his client's investments from lower yield but safer securities to make the purchases. More pointedly, he had been busy diverting Harrison Keeps' investments.

Harrison wept as he heard how Carshalton the company and the man were now bankrupt. Darius had killed the company his great grandfather had started as a blue-collar credit union in the depression era.

Harrison Meeks lost every penny he had invested with them over the years. He had a house, sure, but no-one wanted to buy it from him in this market. Depressed and alone, Harrison Meeks called in at a bar and started drinking. He was still drinking in 2010 when his YouTube account defaulted and was closed.

By that time his content was poor to the point of being unwatchable and he repeatedly refused to observe the new YouTube guidelines.

In a bold effort to boost subscribers Harry sneaked into the abandoned Hard Rock Café in Universal Studios and produced a video showing the deserted space. He was suspended for a month from the parks. Annoyed at the suspension, the next month he doubled down by breaking into the old Triceratops Encounter attraction and filming inside the empty building. He was banned for life from Universal Orlando properties.

Harrison shaved his beard, cut his hair and adopted eccentric glasses in order to obtain a new annual pass in his half-brother's name. He then continued filming but it was all too little too late. The new vloggers were taking over. Before long the media people at Disney lost his number, and after a while, both Universal and Disney asked him to lose theirs. This time in writing from their lawyers.

One by one his sponsors, subscribers and followers deserted him. He was left a broken man, a shadow who wandered about an exquisite old house that took every penny of his dwindling savings to maintain.

Harry took nine years and three spells in rehab, thanks to his family, to wake up to the fact he was killing himself with alcohol and prescription drugs. For heaven's sake, he was still a young man at forty-two years old.

Just as he began to resurface and make an impression on the real world again, in 2020 the pandemic hit. Harrison Meeks was hospitalised and left with a huge medical excess to pay. He returned to his historic house which he had originally called The Raven's Claw and converted it into a high-end bed and breakfast, with the help of his brother.

For the next three years no-one, not even customers, saw or heard from the sick, bitter and very damaged recluse.

Part Two: Today

3
The Holidays are Coming

"Stop surreptitiously sipping that Dayquil syrup. You look like a homeless person drinking from a hip flask," Nikki demanded.

"I'm sick with the flu," Rick argued. Nikki sighed.

"Sick with man flu maybe," she muttered loud enough to be heard. "You can have no possible idea whether you are exceeding the recommended dose."

"It makes me feel better." Rick was feeling less appreciated that he might be, considering his suffering.

"Perhaps we'll stop off on the way home and buy some crack cocaine, I'm sure that will make you feel better still." Rick put the Dayquil away and made a performance out of blowing his nose.

They parked in the preferred parking at Universal Studios. Nikki had been driving. They were parked at the theme park exit level and so, using the moving walkways, they headed directly to the hub for a security check.

As they approached Citywalk Nikki began to feel that she may have been harsh with Rick.

"If we get the update videos done quickly, I'll take you to Confisco's for lunch."

Rick brightened even more quickly than he did after a mouthful of Dayquil.

Now that the Halloween props had been removed Universal Studios was going full on with their Christmas preparations. The tree was up, the red tinsel swags were hung, and Earl the squirrel was concealed in the tree branches.

"Rick, Nikki!" Sue Whitfield, a Vice President of their channel, attracted their attention as the couple filmed the Mummy ride lines; the ride was finally out of technical rehearsal and had a single rider line.

Nikki and Sue hugged; Rick steered clear as he did not want to spread his cold germs.

"Have you received an invite to the First Annual Theme Park Vlogger Awards?" Sue asked, her husband skulking in the background.

"No. The last time we accepted an invitation to a special event we were kidnapped and feared for our lives," Nikki responded. Sue laughed.

"You two and your shenanigans. This is quite safe. Fidus have been asked to be co-sponsors, as we have been publishing the RixFlix/Universal Short Stories all year." She paused. "And, as I sign the cheques, I said Yes."

"We heard rumours..." Rick began before being interrupted by Nikki channelling her inner flashing lights by opening and closing her hands quickly whilst saying Rumour Alert, Rumour Alert. "But no invitation as yet."

"Well as co-sponsor we have seen the short list of nominees and you are nominated in three categories. You will receive an invite soon."

The two couples chatted for a while and parted, agreeing to do lunch soon.

"It looks like you will need to get your old Tux out again," Nikki suggested as they walked towards Chez Alcatraz and Murph.

"And you can wear that expensive blue dress you wore at the media event in January," Rick added. Nikki looked at him. Her expression was not one of total satisfaction. She spoke as she took him by the arm and stopped him in his tracks outside Richter Burger.

"What kind of man would have his wife turn up at an exclusive event like this in a dress everyone has seen before?"

Rick's senses may have been dulled by the cold symptoms, and a pint of Dayquil, but he could spot a trap when he saw one.

"Not this one," he said boldly, adding under his breath "I'm guessing."

For the remainder of the walk around Rick was trying to strategize how he could manoeuvre Nikki towards JC Penney, Macey's at a pinch, but he would try his level best to keep her away from Nordstrom.

"Actually, we could call in at Ross or TK Maxx on the way back, to see what they have." Rick said more in hope than expectation.

Nikki's loud laughter ended that conversation.

***

Rick collapsed into his favourite recliner and took a quick sip of Dayquil whilst Nikki was reorganising her Back to the Future Loungefly backpack. The Airbnb annexe attached to their house was occupied and the current tenants tapped on the adjoining door.

Nikki unlocked it and invited the wife into their kitchen.

"Nikki, the apartment is absolutely perfect," Sandy Brownlow gushed. "And staying close to you and Rick is a dream come true." Nikki smiled. It had been her idea to buy a larger house and fund it with an 'In Law' annexe that could be rented out to their followers and subscribers. The annexe was fully booked now until May next year.

"Here, a messenger delivered this while you were out." Sandy handed Nikki an ornate envelope that probably cost ten dollars on its own. It was of such quality that she would feel guilty about tearing it open.

"Thank you. We have been expecting something. Have a nice evening in the parks. Be sure to check out the Hogwarts Christmas Lightshow."

Nikki opened the envelope carefully, having relocked the connecting door – everyone needs privacy – and took out a beautifully crafted invitation to the Inaugural Vlogger Awards.

They would be attending the event as guests of the organisers. There were only 12 tables, each for two persons. Each table had an allocated bedroom in the venue so that everyone could have a drink and stay the night.

The dinner menu looked amazing. Champagne would be flowing, the awards would be livestreamed, and Chuck Benson from the local News Channel was hosting.

This could be the event that lifted RixFlix to the next level, after something of a let-down at Halloween. It had been exciting enough, and they survived, but the authorities were insistent that the couple kept quiet about their shenanigans until after the trial. Albeit J Jackson Bentley still managed to get a book deal out of their horrifying ordeal.

The RSVP was sent by email a few minutes later.

4
The House by the Lake

If someone threw a hand grenade into the gathered assembly almost the entire Vlogging community of Orlando would vanish from our screens.

The Orlando Informer had organised a pre–Awards Drinks Party at the Hard Rock Café for all of the vloggers who had been included in the vote. Obviously, most overseas vloggers sent their apologies, unless they were nominated, and none had been. The short list consisted entirely of people in the contiguous United States.

Taylor Strickland had ruled himself out of contention early in the nomination process as he was conflicted. Orlando Informer were another of the sponsors alongside Fidus and the park media teams. Nonetheless, he circulated with a drink in his hand, meeting for the first time many people he had met only on social media and by email.

"Rick, somehow I imagined you would own a yellow tuxedo," Taylor joked as he approached a small gathering including Rick and Nikki. Rick laughed. He was wearing a black tuxedo, a cummerbund and a black bow tie, he was taking the black-tie invitation seriously.

Taylor stood back and looked at Nikki. He took in a sharp intake of breath. He was about to say 'you scrub up well' when he thought better of it. "You look simply incredible," he gushed. Nikki frowned with disbelief even though she actually did look incredible. "I am reminded of the moment when Hermione Grainger appears at the top of the staircase, dressed for the Hogwarts Ball."

Nikki's dress by Valenti of London, Paris, Milan and Winter Garden, would have been equally fitting for the red carpet at the Met Gala. It was an all-out, hit 'em in the eye, ball gown. A full-length display of silk taffeta and lace, it merged the pink of Hermione's dress with the blue of Belle's dress gown in Beauty and the Beast. It began at the shoulders and touched the floor, swaying as it moved.

The lady who had prepared Nikki's make-up had complemented her on long hair and had dutifully styled it in manner expected of a 1940's film star.

Nikki playfully punched Taylor lightly on the upper arm to cover her embarrassment at the compliment.

Taylor looked around the gathered group of six and asked, "Has anyone ever met Harrison Meeks? I mean, he is a legend of sorts, but he seems to have been out of the loop for a decade or more."

No-one had heard of Meeks before the invitations landed. Taylor, being a studious fellow, had researched the man. He knew all about Harrison's rise to fame, the crash and his self-imposed exile. Taylor was the only one who had previously stayed at The Raven's Claw Hotel. It was a wonderful period piece. It melded Victoriana and American Restoration architecture and art perfectly. It was filled with dark panelling and wood features; it was cool in the summer and cosy in the winter. Taylor would have liked to stay there again but only twelve rooms were available and there were twelve nominees.

The hotel's only negative was its remoteness. It had the vast lake at the front of the house and dense woodland on the other three sides. No-one would traverse those woods alone. If you did you would soon have snakes, insects and the odd alligator for company. Taylor shuddered involuntarily; he couldn't work out why he had this feeling of foreboding.

***

The list of nominees had been posted on the high-top drinks tables. It read:

1) Alvin Starstruck
2) Doctor in the Parks

3) Florida Florence, FloFlo
4) Mr Who
5) RixFlix
6) Tim Tracker and Jen
7) Mammoth Club Molly
8) Paging Mrs Minniver
9) Devlin D
10) Theme Park Living
11) Morgan and Terry
12) Ears and Beers

There was also an honourable mention of Tom Corless who would also be co-hosting the livestream from the temporary WDWT studio at the Hard Rock Cafe. Tom and his crew were also excluded because they were jointly sponsoring the event.

The nominees were competing for several awards, and each had been nominated more than once. The awards were prize enough; each one had a sharp geometric shape, and was laser etched Austrian Crystal. Around nine inches high, the awards would grace any YouTube studio backdrop.

The trophies were on display at the head table with the list of award categories. They were listed as:

1) Best Overall Theme Park Vlogger
2) Best Universal Orlando Vlogger
3) Best Walt Disney World Vlogger
4) Best Update Vlog
5) Best Ride Vlog
6) Best Food Vlog

Shared equally, which was no guarantee with open voting on the internet, half of the attendees would go to sleep with an award on their hotel bedside table.

If they had ever read an Agatha Christie novel set in a remote venue, they would also know that not everyone would ever go to sleep again!

***

The two limousines pulled away from the valet parking lot at Universal Orlando, filled with nominees and their plus one's. There were six people in each limo, limos that could accommodate double that number. It seemed that the organisers were deliberately trying to impress.

It was six o clock in the evening and the award ceremony would begin streaming at 8pm. The attendees were on their way.

***

"Tom, do you have a minute?" Taylor Strickland asked as he approached his fellow theme park commentator. Tom smiled and said "Sure."

Taylor introduced the lady standing by his side. "Tom, this is Sue, she is CEO of Fidus Press, our co-sponsor." Tom shook the woman's hand. She was a handsome woman, and she must have been close to fifty years old. He had imagined a younger woman, having corresponded with her so frequently over the past month. Sue took the floor.

"Tom, Taylor, you know that our RixFlix books were a runaway success in 2022 and so we anticipated increased interest from the USA. In September we received a formal invitation at our Dallas office from Harrison Meeks to help establish the awards. We were happy to sponsor the event, as were you, and we still are. In fact, I am excited to see what you two handsome young bucks do with the livestream." Both men blushed at once.

"The thing is, I was contacted by a lady claiming to be the former manager of 'The Raven's Claw'. She said that she needed to warn me that Harrison Meeks had an aneurism in the spring and since then he had become a little erratic, she thinks he may be paranoid."

Both men looked concerned.

"But don't worry. He won't be there in person wearing a Michael Myers mask and brandishing a knife, he will be appearing only via a recorded message." Sue paused. "Just in case, I insisted that we have security at the event, ostensibly to keep out fans, but really to make sure all goes according to plan."

"Did you employ the police?" Tom asked.

"More or less. The officer who protected Rick and Nikki Cochrane earlier in the year will be attending in a personal capacity along with Detective John Borgan, one of his colleagues. Don't worry, I'm covering the cost."

Tom and Taylor had their concerns but honestly, who would want to hurt theme park vloggers? In any event Harrison Meeks was a legend, he was a geek, he certainly wasn't the kind of guy who would place his fellow vloggers at risk, would he?

Sue crooked her arms and said, well gentlemen, who is buying me a drink?" They each hooked an arm and walked towards the open bar.

5

A Warm Reception

The beautifully decorated Christmas tree dominated the reception area. It was tall, majestic, and real. Festooned as it was with a thousand lights, there was also room for ornaments depicting Mickey Mouse, Minnie, various princesses, and characters from the Wizarding World.

The remainder of the room was equally well decorated, and a log fire burned ferociously in a large ornate brick fireplace.

Equally welcoming was the smile on the face of the manager. He was clearly delighted to see them all. The name plate on the desk read "Piers K. Roe-Nash", a name more associated with a butler in Downton Abbey, Nikki thought, and his manner was exactly as expected.

Managing to appear deferential whilst acting in a superior fashion was a skill. It was a skill that Mr Roe-Nash had perfected. "What does the K stand for?" Rick asked in a light-hearted manner. Mr Roe-Nash paused long enough to make everyone feel uncomfortable, smiled and then said, "Karyl."

"You can see why I don't advertise the matter." He paused. "My mother was of East European heritage, and it was her Father's name." The man was clearly a highly educated American, but his Mid Atlantic accent owed more to Oxford and Cambridge than to Harvard and Yale.

Rick walked over to the two-seat leather sofa on the far side of the room. Above the sofa was a picture of a Raven flying in to alight on a bare tree branch, its black wings spread wide in flight, its talons sharp and extended.

"It looks like the badge of Ravenclaw House at Hogwarts," he announced to the room.

Mr Roe-Nash sniffed. "Actually, it's an Adolph Dietrich original. He lived from 1877 to 1957 and was one of the most famous Swiss painters of the twentieth century. Long before Ms Rowling created her stories. I imagine that the painting is worth around fifty thousand pounds at auction."

Roe Nash then crossed the room and admired the canvas as he stood beside Rick. "It is dark, enigmatic and threatening, but it has a certain charm."

Rick looked at the man more closely. He was thin, did not look especially healthy and was somewhat pale. An unusual attribute for someone who lived in Central Florida. The man smiled as he saw Rick examining him, but the smile did not reach the eyes. They were a dark blue but away from the direct light they looked decidedly dark, black even.

Over the next few minutes, the keys were distributed to each of the guests, and they were invited to check their rooms and deposit their bags.

The group would gather in the ballroom at 7pm for dinner and drinks, then the awards would be made.

***

Chuck Benson attended to his own make-up; he was appearing on a livestream after all. He was in the main bathroom as he was not staying the night. He practised his smile and hoped that the brightness of his teeth would dazzle the ladies to such a degree that they would not notice the ever-increasing wrinkles, and these darned spots that appeared from nowhere and needed copious amounts of concealer to hide them.

"Chuck, good to see you again," the smartly dressed man said enthusiastically. Chuck Benson was not at all sure that the two had met before. The man extended his hand.

"Dr. Nick Cosgrove, former medical consultant for Channel 12, now a full time vlogger."

Chuck smiled and shook hands. He had a vague recollection of having met the man before. "Good to see you again. I hope to be handing you an award later."

The doctor smiled and then washed his hands. "Can't be too careful with Covid making a comeback!" he said conversationally. "No-one wants to die before their time." It was a throwaway remark but to Chuck it sounded ominous.

6

... And the Winner Is...

The dinner was served on a long dining table in the dining room, an annexe to the much larger ballroom. The outside caterers were efficient and attentive. They ensured that the food was hot when delivered to the table, even though it had been prepared off site.

Then when the meal was over, they cleared the tables as quickly as they had set them, all of the washing up was packed up and taken away in the van that carried the catering staff.

With the limos back at their HQ in Sanford the driveway was empty. The only people in the great hotel were the manager, the twenty-four guests and the compere for the night.

***

The vloggers were heady with wine and engrossed in each other's stories. Laughter rang out from the various groupings as humorous stories about park goers were discussed. Then there was the sound of a gong.

Roe-Nash was ushering everyone into the ballroom. The walls and ceilings were hung with white lace swags which gave the room a romantic feel. The lighting was bright, and the tables were covered with white linen cloths, as were the chair backs.

Each table had place markers carrying the names of the Vloggers. There was a red rose on each table, ostensibly for the partners. The roses were so fragrant that it appeared that the scent had been augmented artificially. Above each table, tethered by a thin ribbon, was a colourful celebratory helium filled balloon with the table number on the front and a picture of the Vlogger on the rear.

***

A few minutes before 8pm the crowd were hushed and Chuck Benson made his entrance. He stood at the back of the room awaiting the livestream. There was a countdown from Mr Roe-Nash and exactly at 8pm the lights became brighter as the host walked to the podium at the front of the ballroom. The podium was bedecked with the sponsors' logos and the backdrop was a set of heavy maroon velvet curtains. The livestream was underway.

The events of the evening were being recorded by two fixed cameras aimed at the podium, and a wide angled go-pro aimed at the vloggers. The cameras were being controlled mainly by AI but with the oversight of pallid but inexpensive young gamer connected by the internet. He was sitting somewhere in Kissimmee, his mum's basement probably.

"Welcome everyone." Chuck Benson's smile had a wattage that could have powered the Griswolds' House in Christmas Vacation.

"I am Chuck Benson from Channel 2 News. You may also recognise me from the award-winning infomercials 'Triton Leaf Blowers, making fall someone else's problem' and 'Dax Grapefruit Smoothies, lose weight and add years to your life'." Chuck paused to allow the online audience time to recall his past work.

"And there's more," he joked, quoting from every TV offer ever made. "I was recently the host of 'The Grouting Contractor's Awards' and the aptly named 'Winnebago Owner of the Year Dinner/Dance.'

But tonight, our worldwide audience is celebrating with us the Orlando Theme Park Vloggers of the Year."

The assembled gathering clapped, but as there were just 24 of them a sleepy young adult in Kissimmee sipped on a Slurpee and added an enhanced applause audio track. To those watching back at Universal Studios and around the world it sounded like Chuck was addressing the audience at Carnegie Hall.

Chuck continued with an icebreaker. "I was a YouTuber, but I was demonetised! It made no cents." There were a few giggles. Encouraged, he continued. "Why do YouTubers like the Legend of Zelda? Because there's always a link in the description."

Rick laughed out loud at that one and Chuck appreciated it.

"Tough audience," Chuck thought to himself. "I'll quit while I'm behind."

***

An hour later five of the six awards had been made and they were now sitting on the tables of the Trackers, RixFlix, Mammoth Club Molly, Devlin D and Mr Who.

Chuck Benson had run dry of witty repartee and was delighted that he would soon be on his way home to a glass of eggnog, his new fleecy pyjamas and where he would be streaming *A New Christmas Story*. He didn't expect a call from his kids, that would be too much to ask, but his ex-wife would call just before midnight to make sure he was OK, as she always did.

"Now for the main Prize of the night! The prestigious "Theme Park Vlogger of the Year Award"! But before that let's hear from the man who started it all almost twenty years ago. Mr Harrison Meeks."

A large flat screen TV flickered into life with a recoded video playing. There, sitting in the lobby of the Raven's Claw Hotel, was the man himself. He was dressed for dinner with a White Tie and tails, snugly fitted around his ample frame. He looked older than his forty-two years, but everyone knew why.

"Hello everyone, you are probably wondering who has won the final award of the night. Well by an international vote and survey conducted on Survey Monkey, the winner is:

He paused to unnecessarily unseal a golden envelope that he himself had sealed earlier.

"Alvin Starstruck."

Everyone was astonished. Alvin had a minor channel and few subscribers for his rather eclectic take on the Disney Parks, he had been thought to be an absolute outsider.

"Thank you and Goodnight everyone." The recorded Harrison Meeks video faded out and the screen showed the three sponsor's logos.

A shocked Alvin Starstruck, real name Dixon Pantsledge, took to the podium and stuttered and stammered his way through an acceptance speech, in much the same way he presented his vlogs.

***

In Kissimmee a concerned gamer who was supposed to be managing the video feed for the Vlogger Awards was flapping. He lost the internet feed as soon as Alvin Starstruck stood. He and the entire livestream universe would miss the finale, the award of the top prize.

Dwayne tried everything, but nothing worked. The internet was still on. He still had a live link. Something had gone wrong with the feed from the Hotel. Having tried everything he was nervous that he would be blamed, or that he would not be paid the rest of his fee. Either way a spliff would help. He lit up, breathed in, and forgot all about Vloggers and their awards.

***

Chuck Benson was standing one side of the stage hoping that this would soon all be over when he saw the curtains rustle behind the podium. Then as they slowly parted, others noticed too.

Out from behind the curtains pointed a handgun, a Glock 19. People looked on in horror as the gun slowly turned to be perpendicular to the curtains. It was pointing at the back of Alvin Starstruck, who would leave this life as Alvin Bulletstruck.

Chuck Benson gauged that if he dived across the stage he could save the life of the Vlogger, but then he reasoned that it would be the wrong decision. It was his responsibility to carry on for his fans; not for himself, but for the army of admirers whose day would be so much darker without him.

No, he would like to dive in and save the man, but he had a public duty to survive this and be there for the viewers.

As he was thinking all of this through, a shot rang out. Alvin shuddered, and blood spilled from his mouth. The screams and shouts were silenced by the large TV screen coming back on.

A laughing Harrison Meeks had recorded an extra segment to his video.

"Well everyone, the first of you is dead. By morning there will be few survivors. Do not try to leave. You all contributed to the ruination of my life and now your lives are mine to take.

The doors and windows are shuttered from the storm, and from escape. Plus. The main doors are chained and armed with C4 explosive.

Use your wits and be brave, and you may survive the night."

As if on demand the thunder clapped and all of the lights went out.

7

We are all in the dark!

Tom Corless, Taylor Strickland and Sue from Fidus were enjoying alcohol free cocktails designed by Murph, the master of his art, and watching the livestream. They were as puzzled as everyone else when the overall winner was announced. "Alvin who?" echoed around the room. And then the screen went blank.

The room groaned as people were disappointed by the blank screens. At least they knew who won, even if they didn't know who he was.

The tech people ran around for a few minutes checking lines and calling providers. A lady call Andrea came and sat at the sponsors' table.

"It must be the storm. It's over the lake. Not only have we lost the internet link, but the mobile phones are down too. It's possible that it's a power outage. We are doing what we can but our live link expires in five minutes anyway.

We will put out an apology just before the link is disconnected but we had several thousand streaming and we are down to just fifteen hundred already."

No-one at the table was worried. The hotel was safe and secure, it was hurricane protected and had standby generators. The Vloggers would be fine.

***

Things did not seem fine to the 24 people in the hotel. There were twelve main Vloggers in attendance, a further eight partners (four vloggers teamed up together in two partnerships), two security men, the hotelier and Chuck Benson.

Each of them were concerned, worried that they may be next on the list and panicked by the sudden darkness. Phone lights and zippo lighters offered crude local illumination.

"Someone find the board," a voice pleaded as the emergency lighting kicked in. Everyone breathed a sigh of relief.

Doctor Don Clements (Dr in the Parks- Vlogger) was kneeling over the stricken body of Alvin. He ordered everyone to stay back.

After a few moments he announced that Alvin Starstruck was dead.

The two security men had been busy checking the doors and windows. They were all secured and the main doors, front and back, had suspicious wires leading under them and outside.

"Secure the gun," Detective John Borgan demanded of Officer Ray Dalton, as the Doctor covered the body with a spare black tablecloth.

The gun had reverted to its place behind the curtain and was secured to the wall by a complex swinging bracket, controlled by an electrically operated actuator.

The gun was tack welded to steel bracket and so he slid out the magazine, having checked that there was no chambered round. The gun was empty. There had been only one round in the gun.

Officer Dalton examined the contraption that had just killed a vlogger. It was hinged and fastened to the wall. It could be swung out to ninety degrees but no more. At that angle the bracket was fully extended.

The Detective and Officer Dalton looked more closely.

"Look at this wire," Dalton said. "It's looped around the trigger. When the bracket is flat against the wall, the wire is loose. As the bracket swings out it tightens until at ninety degrees…"

The Detective finished the thought.

"It pulls the trigger and we have a dead award winner." He paused and looked around, addressing the vloggers who were visibly upset and concerned.

"According to my count everyone in this hotel is in this room. We have four to eight hours of power, if we use it sparingly, from the standby generators.

Now, it may seem bleak but if we all stay together no harm will befall us. Officer Dalton and I are sworn law officers, and we are armed." Officer Dalton shook his head vigorously.

"Well, one of us is armed. Mr Roe-Nash, please help the doctor move the body to the small changing room behind the curtain and lock the changing room door. Oh, and keep the key safe."

Roe-Nash obliged. When he reached the stage area he made an impromptu speech.

"Were it not for a dead body I would assume that this was some kind of a sick prank, but not only is the power out, the phones are too." The beginnings of what may have been panic tinged his voice. "The cell phone mast may have been struck by lightning again, just as it was during Hurricane Ian a couple of months back.

We're all stuck here together until morning, so please do as the Detective says. Let's stay safe."

The Doctor and Roe-Nash removed the body and returned with the room key.

"Listen everyone." The hubbub declined as the Detective shouted. "Mr Starstruck was killed by a mechanical arm. That has been disabled. We are safe now. No one can get in or out.

Even if we could get out it is over a mile and a half to the main road and that is often deserted on a fine night, let alone in a storm. The nearest house is almost two miles away through the woods, and the woods have all kinds of nasties in them; snakes, wild animals, even alligators. So, lets stay calm. We have food, we have drink, we have warmth. Let's stick together until we decide what to do next."

There was silence for the next few minutes before Molly from the Mammoth Club called everyone's attention to the Vlogger Wall of Fame.

Here there were photos of all twelve of the Vloggers framed and mounted on the wall in four rows of three. Except that this was no longer the case. The photo of Alvin Starstruck was missing. It had been removed.

Everyone took in a sharp intake of breath as they realised that there was no other explanation. The murderer was one of them.

8

Walking towards the light.

Everyone was sitting nervously at their tables, with drinks in their hands. The two policemen were in a huddle and Mr Roe-Nash was wandering around trying to calm people.

Tim Tracker and Jen pulled their chairs over to the RixFlix table and spoke in hushed tones.

"Rick, Nikki, we don't know each other well but I think we know each other well enough to know that we are not the murderers." Tim spoke urgently but softly. He just wanted to be home with their little boy. "So, I suggest that we stick together, strength in numbers and all that, and see if we can work out which madman is responsible for all of this. After all, you have put away several criminals this year alone without missing a Vlog!"

Rick was thinking, inappropriately, that he would quite like that brilliantined head of hair. He found himself twirling an imaginary moustache like Tim's. Nikki nudged him in the ribs.

"Yes, we agree. We have been in tougher situations. This has been a tricky year. I feel like Miss Marple, tripping over bodies wherever we turn." He chuckled. No-one else did.

Jen remarked, "Fabulous dress, Nikki. By the way." Nikki gave Jen a hug and said "OK. We're in. What should we do next?"

***

Sue, Tom and Taylor had all been on their phones constantly for a quarter of an hour. Sue was still listening when the others set down their phones. She lifted a finger to draw their attention and then set down her phone on the table.

"OK. Simon, you are on speaker."

Simon was a forensic investigator back in London. He was second in command at Vastrick Security London Office, reporting to the quite famous Dee Hammond. The lady who saved a prince during an attack on the Queen's Platinum Jubilee celebrations.

Simon was happy to help even though it was after midnight in the UK. He loved his mum but he did spend a lot of time on the phone resetting Windows on her laptop and helping her recover her lost passwords.

"I have been through all of the data available and on some private data that we will never mention again.

It seems that Harrison Meeks was allowed home in the summer from a private institution in New England. He seemed to be coping but he had an episode and tracked down, and attacked, a man he knew long ago. The man, who is not named in the records, suffered a fractured skull. He was once Meek's banker.

The police report says he was yelling, 'He is just the first, I'll kill them all' before he was sedated by a private nurse.

He was bailed to a secure facility to await trial until he escaped two weeks ago. The facility thought he was hiding out in New Hampshire. He is thought to be a homicidal paranoic.

He's a very dangerous man. He can appear calm and normal whilst killing without remorse."

"Simon, where is he now? Could he be in Orlando?" Tom Corless asked.

"I think it's likely. He has property there and the people he perceives have stolen his livelihood all live there."

***

Paging Mrs Miniver was a jolly fellow, well-loved and always happy. A single murder was not going to deter him. He was going to raise everyone's spirits.

"Mr Roe- Nash. Can't we do something to lift the mood?" he asked.

"Well, sir, you all have a helium balloon, filled with laughing gas. Silly voices always amuse."

Paging Mrs Miniver (Errol to his mother) sucked in a mouthful of gas and stood up. "Hello, welcome to Chip'n'Dales magical world," he yelled in a falsetto voice. Everyone giggled and soon balloons were being taken down and their necks loosened.

Tim, Jen, Rick and Nikki looked on as those around them, mostly single young adults, had fun.

The younger ones encouraged everyone to join in. "Come on, Doc. Give it a go," Ears and Beers yelled.

The Doctor wanted to point out the foolishness of inhaling helium gas but thought, 'What the heck', and drew in a large breath.

Everyone was listening to what he would say. Would he do his famous Donal Duck impression? He opened his mouth, but no sound came out. He began to choke. Panic spread across his face and his hands were at his throat. He couldn't breathe. He ripped open his collar button and loosened his tie. All to no avail. As he collapsed onto the table before sliding to the floor, he managed one word:

"Murder!"

***

The doctor was dead. There was no doubt. His face was contorted, and his eyes stared accusingly. 'You should have saved me'.

"This is crazy. We don't have two murders a month in this jurisdiction, let alone two in one hour," Officer Dalton commented as they leaned over the second dead body of the night.

"They were pre-arranged and so, theoretically, they could have been planned and executed by someone who is not here. We're right back where we started."

A scream emanated from the lobby where FloFlo was staring up at the blogger wall. "He has disappeared too!" she cried, somewhat hysterically.

The group gathered around the Vlogger Wall of Fame. The picture of Doctor in the Park had disappeared. Everyone looked at everyone else. The tension was palpable.

No-one dared say what was running through their minds. 'The person standing next to me may be a killer, a sociopathic killer who is showing no remorse whatsoever."

***

Tom, Sue and Taylor had gathered a few people and were holding a council of war.

"We have just heard from the nearest neighbours to the Raven's Claw, Tammy reached out to them, and they have not lost power or cell phone signal. Yet neither cell phones nor land line are getting through.

We have to assume that something is wrong. We need to call the police, now."

"Can we jump in a car and go and see for ourselves?" Tom asked. "I have a Jeep Wrangler, it can handle anything." Taylor looked at Sue and they agreed that they should do something. They set off for valet parking after calling the police.

***

"No, no, no. Not again. I'm not having this. Give it to Polk County, Lake County, Orlando Police or the damned FBI!" the Police Chief yelled as everyone cowered.

"Rick and Nikki, Nikki and Rick. They have orchestrated a two Vlogger crimewave across my county all year. First a bloodthirsty serial killer, then a crazy half-ass car chase and half my budget spent on recovering them from a crazed woman killer in Flagstaff.

Where is officer Dalton? Call Dalton, he's their stooge."

No-one wanted to say what they all knew. He was at the Raven's Claw offering security out of hours.

After a minute the Chief calmed himself with a sip of his chamomile tea. "OK. Send a car and an armed response unit.

This is Rick and Nikki Cochrane we are talking about. They have been escalating all year. They are probably involved in a drug war, or have stumbled on a major terrorist threat." He paused as people swung into action. "I'm minded to call in the FBI as well," he muttered under his breath.

9

One more shock.

Chuck Benson had allied himself to the largest of the three groups now sitting together in the ballroom. No-one was taking their eyes off their companions.

He could hardly believe that this was all real. The Detective said that the Doctor's balloon had been filled with a foul-smelling gas, probably mixed in with the helium. He suspected it was cyanide gas, given the speed of reaction and the symptoms.

When the Vloggers heard that the gas had been doctored, they let their balloons go. Several balloons flew around the room at once, making noises previously acquainted with comedy cushions or baked bean eating cowboys in a Mel Brooks movie.

Jen, Tim, Rick and Nikki had been joined by Officer Dalton. The remaining Vloggers had split into two groups, one headed by Mr Roe-Nash, and one now headed by Chuck Benson.

Chuck liked to be in charge, but he didn't like the responsibility of leadership, nor was he qualified for leadership. So, Molly took the chair. She was running through what they could do to protect themselves until help arrived in the morning, when Chuck remembered that he had a bottle of whisky in a gift bag beside his briefcase. It was from the sponsors. A thoughtful gift.

He excused himself and then concealed himself behind a column as he stripped off the foil cover and broke the seal of the exclusive twelve-year-old single malt from Scotland. This whisky was too good to share. He poured a generous two fingers of the amber nectar into a glass and savoured the aroma. It was smoky and fragrant. He began to salivate.

He quickly downed the whisky, its bouquet tantalising his taste buds before the liquid warmed the back of his throat. He resealed the bottle and placed it back in the gift bag.

As he walked back to the table, he felt a pain in his abdomen. It quickly rose to his chest, where it developed into an agonising seizure. He knew that he was in trouble when the top of his left arm was engulfed in agony too.

He collapsed onto the floor beside his tablemates.

Detective John Borgan rushed over. "He isn't breathing." He checked the man's pulse. "If he has a pulse, I'm not feeling it. I'm starting CPR."

He tried CPR without success and Officer Dalton offered to take over. "Wait, there's a defibrillator on the wall," a man's voice shouted above the din. Officer Dalton raced to the wall and quickly read the instructions.

"Great news," he said. "It's the same as the one we carry in our vehicles. I've used it before."

In a few seconds he had it ready to go. "OK everyone, stand back." He placed the paddles on the newsreader's bare chest, as instructed, and pressed the red button.

There followed a loud bang. Officer Dalton was flung three metres away and the newsman's body briefly caught fire. Three people fainted at the smell of burning flesh.

***

Officer Dalton was recovering by the wall, his back against the wall and his feet extended. Nikki was feeding him sips of chilled water as his own hands were shaking.

He had no serious injuries that he could fathom, but he had a terrible headache.

"The defib machine was tampered with. This has to be another murder," the detective whispered as he knelt down by his brother officer. "The whisky is almost certainly laced with something, probably Methamphetamine. It has no smell and so we will need a tox screen to confirm." He paused and looked at the still smoking body of the newscaster. At least it had been covered with another tablecloth.

"The whisky was supposed to be a gift from the sponsors and as it was sealed, he thought it was safe. There is a tiny hole in the lid that has been clumsily resealed."

"You think it was injected by a syringe?" Nikki asked.

"I can think of no better explanation. Look, we need to be proactive. Hiding away and being reactive is just causing death after death."

"The Vlogger wall of fame!" Rick exclaimed suddenly almost running to the reception area. When he arrived, predictably, the poster advertising the event with Chuck's photo and name had been defaced. The photo of the man's face had been cut into pieces by a knife.

"I don't get it, Rick, "Tim Tracker said quietly. We were watching the whole time, and no-one left the room."

"I know, Tim. There is someone else in this building." He paused as he gathered the courage to speak the words.

"And he is picking us off one at a time."

10

You are on your own.

The Blue Jeep Wrangler emblazoned with the WDWNT logos worked its way slowly along the I4. Florida drivers hated rain and when it fell in a torrential manner they slowed almost to a stop. At this rate it would take two hours to get to the Raven's Claw and by then the police and the emergency power crews would probably have restored order. Tom, Taylor and Sue were harbouring second thoughts but not voicing them.

Theirs appeared to be a forlorn journey but they continued for the sake of their friends. It was 10pm and the sky was ominous. The chances of Rick and Nikki being involved in another life-or-death situation were astronomically low, but they all knew that these two Vloggers seemed to attract ne'er-do-wells.

***

Officer Dalton had three bodies in storage. The first in the dressing room behind the stage, and two in the walk-in freezer in the kitchen.

"I'm thinking that we should bring Alvin's body in here too," he thought out loud.

"No, the dressing room is unheated, it will be fine there. We don't want to tip the Vloggers over the edge with the sight of another dead body so soon after the demise of Mr Benson," Mr Roe-Nash answered.

"I guess you're right," the policeman conceded. Was that relief he saw wash over the manager's countenance? No, surely not. He was tired and imagining things. It had been a tough night.

Officer Dalton wandered over to the corner of the room where the Cochranes and the Trackers were plotting something.

"Ray, we have been thinking about the events of the night so far and we have summarised our thoughts as follows. Jen and Nikki." The two girls had written a list on an Orlando Informer notebook. Two had been left at every table with two wdwnt.com pens and a couple of Fidus mouse mats.

"Well, first all three murders to date have been set up earlier, pre-planned so to speak. So, the Hotel must be involved somehow," Jen said, her blue eyes earnestly locked on those of Officer Dalton. Nice eyes, framed by blonde hair, Ray's favourite combination. "Get a grip," he thought. "She is married, and you are investigating three murders."

"I agree," Nikki chimed in. "You can't install a heavy bracket like the one holding the gun without some serious tools and a couple of guys."

Dalton nodded.

"Then there's the balloon set up. We assume only one had poison gas, so it must have been pre-arranged as the balloons have names and pictures on them." Nikki finished speaking and handed back to Jen.

"Finally, the defibrillator was so damn obvious, it was right there on the wall in plain view. Usually there would be a discreet sign pointing to an alcove somewhere, but this was a bright red eyesore on a pristine, turn of the century wallpaper." Nikki came back with a final point.

"The pictures of the Vloggers, and poor old Chuck Benson, they weren't removed by us, we were all in view of each other. There is someone else here. Find him or her and we find our killer."

The small group were pondering these points when Detective Borgan joined them. He must have overheard the conversation because he had one more point to add.

"What about the voice that directed me to the tricked-out defibrillator?" They had all quite forgotten that a male voice had directed their attention to the red box on the wall. "Does anyone recall who said it?"

They all thought back. It had seemed at the time like a local accent, a little bit of the south with mid-American overtones. It sounded much like

Chuck Benson but he was on the floor being treated. Tim Tracker jumped in.

"We have all seen and heard the nominees a thousand times. We would recall who it was if it was them. Although Morgan's husband Terry rarely speaks and so we probably wouldn't recognise his voice. Morgan and Terry were a delightful couple both young and handsome, well dressed and groomed in the way that only metropolitan men seem able to achieve.

"What about the manager Mr Piers K Roe-Nash? He has that odd mid Atlantic accent, which must be affected. I wonder what his real accent sounds like?"

"It would be handy if the K stands for Killer," Rick joked. No-one laughed.

"It stands for Karyl, we asked him," Nikki said to curb her husband's embarrassment.

"Well, we have some investigating to do, but stay in our eyeline at all times. We don't want to lose anyone else," the detective said ominously.

11

Universal Orlando's Hollywood Boulevard has the answer!

Everyone was tired. The remaining vloggers and their partners were dead on their feet. Terror and fear had been overwhelmed by weariness and exhaustion. The night had been emotionally draining.

"We need to get these people to their rooms and lock the doors. Then a few of us could patrol the corridors. If we do that everyone should be safe as there will always be more than one person to a room."

The detective was careful in phrasing his words. He did not want Roe-Nash to think that he was under suspicion. They needed to give the man rope to hang himself, if indeed he was the culprit.

The next thirty minutes was spent organising people into rooms of four, where possible. There were now two ladies without partners in the group and they were being cared for by FloFlo and Paging Mrs Miniver, who seemed to have a close, very close, if platonic relationship.

FloFlo took her small flock upstairs under the watchful eye of Officer Dalton. He saw them settled in her room and advised the four people to bolt the door from inside. And maybe prop a chair under the handle, just in case. They did as he asked. Fifteen minutes later the three women were asleep and Gez (Mr FloFlo) sat upright in his chair watching over them.

The other rooms were equally carefully filled and instructed. The last remaining room of the six four person rooms would house the Trackers, Rick and Nikki but they were locked in conversation in the reception.

Officer Dalton sat on a chair at the end of the second-floor corridor from where he could see every occupied room door and the stairs. He was nursing Detective Borgan's trusty handgun, A Sig Sauer P226.

If he remained vigilant everyone would be safe until the storm had passed and daylight returned. As he relaxed in his chair the lights flickered, went off and came back on.

***

"It's the generator. It has switched over to its reserve tank. We need to conserve power, now," Roe- Nash declared to the five people remaining in the reception area.

The message was passed around upstairs by Officer Dalton and soon all bedrooms were illuminated only by a single low wattage table lamp.

The downstairs lights had been turned off. Even the Christmas tree was dark. One ceiling light and the light from the fire made the place seem cosy, warm and safe, but it wasn't.

"I have taken possession of all of the spare keys. I have them here in this bag." Borgan displayed a thick canvass bag that had once been used to take cash to the bank. It rattled with real metal keys jangling.

"Now," he continued, "I am going to search this hotel and find our extra guest. You stay here, stay together. And keep an eye on Roe-Nash, he is still a suspect." The Detective rose and said loudly, "I'm going upstairs to talk to Officer Dalton. You five stick together like glue."

However, as soon as he was out of sight of Roe-Nash and the others he detoured into the empty ballroom and began a grid search of the ground floor.

***

Whilst Tim and Rick were happy to speculate and try to work out who was doing the killing by conversing, their two partners felt that action was needed.

"I have an idea," Nikki whispered to Jen conspiratorially. Jen nodded her head. It was clearly a good idea.

The idea was simple. Roe-Nash was nursing a hot cup of tea, waiting for it to cool enough to drink. Nikki would bump into him and spill the hot drink. He would bellow involuntarily, as men do, and they would hear his real accent.

It took some manoeuvring, but Nikki managed to find a position where she was close to the butleresque manager.

"Oops, Sorry!" she cried as the tea flew everywhere. She had been a little enthusiastic with her nudge. Hot tea spilled on the man's shirt front, his neck, chin and cheek.

"Damnit all, woman! Be more careful!" There it was, his ordinary unaffected voice. All four of the Vloggers now knew who had shouted "There's a defibrillator on the wall'.

A moment later the mid-Atlantic accent was back and he was apologising as much for his outburst as Nikki was for the collision. Roe-Nash ran to his private room behind reception, holding his neck and chin.

***

John Borgan had systematically cleared the ground floor using the small emergency LED flashlight he always kept on his belt. The only room left was the dressing room which contained the body of the first victim. He searched the bag for the spare key, found it and unlocked the door.

He opened the door and looked around the small room before pointing his torch floorward.

He swore out loud. The body had gone and yet the room had been locked all night. He was formulating an outlandish theory when a blow to the back of his head sent him sprawling to the floor, unconscious.

***

Roe-Nash looked in the bathroom mirror. The hot tea had damaged the make-up applied to his neck. The make-up had melted and was hanging from his neck and chin, looking ready to drop at any moment.

He remembered hearing in school that in the 1960 Presidential Debate the same happened to Richard Nixon. His make-up drooped under the studio lights and would have been obvious viewed in profile. So, he spent the whole debate facing the camera. Kennedy noted his discomfiture and kept challenging him to "Look at me." The teacher said that the debate, and the flawed make-up, probably changed the direction of the whole USA, after the wafer-thin Kennedy victory.

Roe-Nash repaired the make up as best he could but it was unsightly and so he wrapped a bandage around his neck to cover the mess and covered that with a scarf that completely filled the gap between his chest and chin.

***

When Roe-Nash returned to the reception desk with his scarf around his neck, Tim whispered, "He is going over the top, isn't he? It was only a splash of tea."

Nikki shouted out. "Sorry, it was my fault." Roe-Nash just raised a hand in acknowledgement and smiled. But his face creased in an odd way. Perhaps he really was in pain.

Tim Tracker looked at the man and shook his head. Roe-Nash had a fake accent and was somehow involved in all of this murder and mayhem.

In a fleeting moment of what Tim would call brilliance and Jen would call common sense, he said out loud, "Scooby Doo."

Everyone looked at him strangely.

12
It's obvious when you already know the answer.

Detective John Borgan was brought back into consciousness by smelling salts, an old fashioned but effective remedy. He shook his head. He was sitting on a chair in the dressing room. There was a silhouette of a man in the doorway.

Borgan faked a coughing fit, bent double and reached for his ankle.

"Don't bother detective, I'm pointing your own ankle gun at you as we speak." The voice was recognisable, but it was impossible at the same time. He was groggy and dazed. He must be mistaken.

But he wasn't.

The man closed and locked the door and flicked on the light.

Standing not three feet from the detective was Alvin Starstruck.

***

Tim Tracker gathered the others and said, "Let's sit close to the fire." He hoped that they would be out of earshot of the manager who was pretending to busy himself behind the bar.

"What is the running joke in Scooby Doo?" he asked.

"The caretaker was always the villain?" Rick queried.

"Absolutely, now what if that is what is happening here? What if our hotel manager is, as we all suspect, involved? Who is he really?" The other three vloggers looked puzzled.

"We have guessed, perhaps even proven, that he is involved, but how can we prove it?" Nikki asked.

"We don't have to. The arrogant turd has been parading his real identity in front of us all night."

***

John Borgan blinked several times before his brain would believe his eyes. Alvin Starstruck was looking on with some amusement.

"But you were shot. The Doctor checked your pulse. He said you had been shot through the heart. You were dead. The blood..."

Alvin laid down the gun and raised his hands to his face. Placing one hand behind his head he pulled at his hair. The Alvin Starstruck wig, dressed in the shape of a 1980's mullet, lifted off easily, leaving a shaved head behind. He laid down the wig that had also removed some latex and a piece of forehead prosthetic. He then proceeded to remove the remainder of the latex along with a nose shaper.

When he was done, he smiled. "Sally, get me the first aid box." He shouted the comedic catchphrase to no-one in particular. John Borgan was stunned.

The role of Alvin Starstruck was being played by none other than Tim Freeman of 'Going Downhill', a modern prime time TV comedy about a dysfunctional Californian family.

Tim Freeman, his stage name, had appeared for several years as the much-loved accident prone character Clumsy Clem, until he was accused of molestation during the *Me Too* period. The two unstable actors who had made the accusations later withdrew their statements, but it was too late for Tim Freeman. No-one would offer him a part again. He had been falsely accused and deprived of an income and career.

"The Doctor was persuaded that we were trying to uncover a murderer and that we needed his help. For a doctor he was really quite dim. He took the line and played his part. As for the rest, well I had a fake blood capsule in my mouth and a squib under my shirt. When both were activated I looked to all the world like a dead man. The gun fired a blank round.

We had to get rid of the Doctor next. There was no telling if and when he would break down and spill the whole story," Borgan interjected.

"That was all set up before the night began. It was premeditated. You knew you would be killing him before you involved him in your plot."

"Yes, well Harry, sorry Harrison Meeks, was convinced that he would have made a comeback as chief theme park vlogger, had it not been for the Doctor and the other usurpers." He paused. "Me, I'm not so sure. I think his time was up anyway."

"Why would you join in his madcap scheme? Killing people. That's dark stuff," John Borgan asked sincerely. The look on Freeman's face changed in an instant. There was madness in his eyes.

"I was famous, I was rich, I was somebody in Hollywood, the hardest place in the world to make your name. I was first choice for two movie roles that would have rocketed me to fame. Instead, they went to Ryan Reynolds.

Look at him now. He can pick his own movies, make cameo appearances, he has a vodka company, and he owns a soccer club. That could have been me," he was yelling. Then he broke down and tears streamed down his face.

"That should have been me," he said quietly as he shed tears for what he had lost and what may have been.

***

"Look, let's just ask ourselves, who is the architect of tonight's tragedy?" Tim whispered.

"Harrison Meeks." Rick, Nikki and Jen responded in unison.

"Correct. Is anyone good at crosswords?" Tim asked oddly. There were no takers. "Anagrams then?" Nikki and Jen both said "So, so."

"Look at Roe Nash's nameplate and what do you see?"

Everyone looked at the polished wooden placeholder with a chromium nameplate slid in to the two rebated edges. It read proudly: Piers K Roe-Nash, Manager.

The girls were there first but Rick got there soon after.

"The letters of Piers K Roe-Nash can be re-arranged to spell Harrison Keeps," Jen exclaimed quietly.

Piers K Roe-Nash stepped out from behind the fireplace and grinned. His face crinkled. "I wondered how long it would take you to figure it out." He was pointing a gun at them.

Roe- Nash removed the scarf to reveal patchy makeup and the edges of a latex mask. He pulled at the bottom of the latex mask and the fake skin peeled off like it did for Doc Brown in Back to the Future 2.

They sat there looking at Harrison Keeps, thinner and paler than he was on the video, but it was most certainly the aging Vlogger, in whose hotel they were resident.

Possibly forever.

13

The end of all Things

When Sue, Taylor and Tom arrived at the Raven's Claw they could hardly get near the place. There were flashing blue and red lights all around.

An officer with a semi-automatic rifle approached them. "Taylor Strickland, I recognise you from YouTube. It seems your tip off was good. The doors and windows are all locked and boarded up against the storm but we found this note on the main door."

"DO NOT ENTER. ALL ENTRANCES BOOBY TRAPPED. C4 DEPLOYED."

"Sadly, they aren't bluffing. The Dog's Nose confirmed the presence of explosives on the main door." The Dog's Nose was a crude term used by Police to describe a TPM, Trace Portal Machine, used for sniffing out drugs and explosives.

"Stay in the car until we tell you it is safe to exit."

Sue's phone rang. It was Simon, it was three in the morning where he was but he sounded bright and alert. The phone was on speaker.

"Mum. Please be careful. I hacked into the rehab centre's records. Meeks has been attending weekly Chemo sessions at the hospital. They have stopped them as they are doing no good. The man has weeks to live, if that.

Don't mess with him, he has nothing to lose."

The three people in the car all shuddered. Explosives, hostages and a man destined to die before Mardi Gras. Not a good mix. The vloggers and their partners were all in deadly danger.

***

Officer Dalton's eyes snapped open. He had fallen asleep. He hoped that it had just been a few seconds and that he hadn't missed anything. He stood and walked across the landing and stood outside each door. Apart from gentle snoring the rooms were silent and calm.

In the semi darkness Ray thought he could see red and blue flashing lights. He opened the heavy drapes. The windows were shuttered on the outside but through their imperfect fit he could see police lights.

He grinned widely and started to descend the stairs. As he got halfway down he heard the voice from the video.

"I am going to take care of you four first and then I will go upstairs and take the other Vloggers down one at a time. I have plenty of ammunition and a suppressor."

Ray stopped dead in his tracks. The four Meeks was referring to would be the Trackers and Cochranes. Everyone else was accounted for upstairs. But where had Meeks come from? Where was Detective Borgan? It was all so confusing for a man who was so recently roused from sleep.

Ray was no hero, but he had to act. He had a gun too. He descended the stairs silently, aided by the thick luxurious carpeting. Before he arrived in the reception area he peeked through the balusters on the old staircase. Meeks had his back to Ray and was pointing a gun at the others.

***

"Up you get, Mr Detective. We are going to meet up with your friends. Nosy sods that they are."

Borgan stood and reluctantly walked towards reception, being prodded in the back by the barrel of his own gun if he faltered.

As they closed in on the reception area, he spotted Ray Dalton on the stairs peeking through the balusters. Tim Freeman's hand covered his mouth before he could issue a warning and the gun was pointed at his temple. With his hands tied behind his back he had few options.

Officer Dalton yelled.

"OK Meeks, drop the gun. Armed Police. You are in my sights, I am less than three metres away I won't miss from here. Your brains will be all over that wall if I get to a three count. One... Two..."

Ray had no intention of shooting Meeks but he hoped that Meeks did not appreciate the fact.

"Ahem." Freeman said loudly. "Put the gun down or your detective friend dies."

"Clumsy Clem?" Dalton stammered. This night got crazier by the minute. He lowered the gun and set it down on the stairs, before descending to the ground level.

***

Five minutes later Rick, Nikki, Tim and Jen were seated facing the two gunmen. The two policemen were tied back-to-back on their chairs with cummerbunds; luckily some people had taken Black Tie seriously. The policemen were immobile.

Harrison Meeks had attached a suppressor to his gun, a Glock 19 with an eleven-round magazine, as the vloggers looked on, all hope lost. Meeks put some powder on the back of his hand and sniffed it up into his nose. He handed the silver box to Freeman, who did the same.

It would take courage and chemicals to enable them to take another dozen lives without faltering.

"Put that pea shooter away," Meeks said about the 38mm ankle gun that Detective Borgan used as a back-up piece. Freeman took out the bullets, pocketed them and slid the useless gun back into its ankle holster on the Detective's leg, laughing as he did so.

"OK. Mr RixFlix, or whatever your real name is, you go first." Meeks raised the gun and aimed. Reluctant to go quietly Rick bravely leapt up as his wife sobbed loudly.

He was barley off the seat when there was the deafening sound of gunfire. The sound echoed around the room and before the retort had died down Rick Cochrane landed hard back in his seat, his face a mask of blood.

14

Happy Holidays, for some.

The police heard the sound of gunfire and the Captain shouted, "Breach, breach'.

Simultaneously the gathered SWAT team crashed through the windows surrounding the reception area. There had been no sign of explosives on the windows and so the risk assessment team had decided to penetrate the perimeter, even before the gunshot.

As the men crashed through the windows, they could see that they were too late. A dead body lay at the feet of Nikki Cochrane and Jen Tracker, as Tim Tracker looked on.

***

Gez Flores, Mr FloFlo, saw blue lights through the window, the light was spilling in around the shutters. He needed to tell Ray Dalton.

Carefully and silently, he unlocked and opened the door. When he looked out Dalton had gone. Gez closed the door, locked it, pocketed the key and set off in search of the policeman.

He was halfway down the stairs when he heard the talking. The policemen were tied up and the vloggers were being kept in their seats by an armed man that might have been Meeks or Roe-Nash, he couldn't be sure. Also, with his back to Gez, was another balding man who was new to the group.

When the gunman made it clear that he intended to shoot everyone, Gez began to panic. Everyone included him and his beloved Florence. She was brash and noisy at times but he lived for her.

He was wondering what to do when he spotted the gun sitting on the stair below his feet. It was a Sig Sauer P226. He picked it up. He recalled from his time in Afghanistan that the gun had no external safety feature.

He had to take a chance that it was loaded and ready to go. If he checked, the noise could alert the gunman and his companion.

When Rick Cochrane was threatened, Gez raised his gun and took aim. As Rick stood Gez knew that he had to act. He fired. His aim had not deteriorated in the two years since he had last fired a gun. The first shot entered Meeks head at the back and exited through his face. The bullet carried on and buried itself in the wall.

Rick was sprayed with Meeks blood, and other things. He was clearly traumatised and sank back into the chair as he passed out. He would recall that moment forever, but Gez reckoned it was better than dying.

The Vloggers were hugging and comforting each other as Gez approached the other man, whose eyes were wide with fear and whose pupils were wide with drugs.

Gez hit the man hard on the temple with the butt of his gun. Freeman fell to the floor, out for the count. Gez was releasing the two policemen when all hell broke loose as the windows came in and bodied appeared yelling "Armed Police".

***

Tom Corless, Taylor Strickland and Sue Whitfield were allowed into the house soon after SWAT had cleared it of explosives. There was a tiny amount of C4 deployed, just enough to blow the doors off.

They each did what they could to placate and comfort the witnesses of the night's events.

Lucinda, who had accompanied Alvin Starstruck to the awards ceremony, confessed that she was an escort, bought and paid for. She had first set eyes on the man tonight at the Universal Studios pre awards drinks meetup.

Doctor in the Parks had been accompanied by Bella Carmody, a beautiful young Tik Tok model who wanted to boost her channel ratings and who cared little for the man who was twice her age and then some.

Everyone else was pleased that they could go home with their partners.

Poor old Chuck Benson had done nothing more to deserve an early death than report the facts about Meeks rehab and his decline into drugs and bankruptcy, a fact he would have had to be reminded of as he had broadcast over 3,000 such stories in his long career.

Milly, his executive assistant, would be asked to tidy up his affairs and find a home for his cat. An ex-wife who cared for him still would get nothing but the two sons who cared nothing for their Dad would get an equal share of his estate and life insurance.

It seemed inevitable that Tim Freeman would serve a life sentence, a lot of it under suicide watch.

Gradually everyone filtered out. Taxi's, Ubers and limos turned up to take everyone home or to hospital for a check-up. As they left, Taylor, Tom and Sue promised them all that they would organise a proper awards event in 2023, noting that every award had been left behind. No-one wanted a reminder of tonight on their bookshelf, albeit Mister Who had been quite keen to take his Best Food Vlog Trophy until peer pressure prevailed.

It was just a few days until Christmas and everyone was already emotionally drained and a physical wreck.

14

A Winter Garden Winter

The Christmas trees were up, decorations adorned every nook and cranny of the main house, and the guest wing was, thankfully, empty.

Rick was relaxing in the hot tub, a serious drink in his hand. He would get past this latest trauma as he had the others. Bright and breezy Rick would be back reporting from the parks the day after Christmas.

Tonight, the couple would be at EPCOT to see the Candlelight Processional, the dinner and reserved seats courtesy of Orlando Informer and WDWNT.

The family would be together for a wonderful Christmas Day feast and life would get back to normal as subscriber numbers rose. It seemed that everyone wanted to see what 2023 would bring for RixFlix. After all, they couldn't possibly anticipate the same shenanigans as this year, could they?

"Nikki." Rick shouted into the main house from the Lanai. "Where's the DayQuil? I'm feeling a little stuffed up.

"I'll be there in a minute," Nikki replied in a sweet voice whilst she was filling up the biggest jug she could find with iced water.

Rick was about to find out what COLD really felt like.

Previous JJB Titles.

J Jackson Bentley is a renowned thriller writer and a member of the International Thriller Writers, where he is listed alongside Lee Child, Jeffrey Deaver, Karen Slaughter and many others. He writes in the UK, and the USA.

The City of London Thrillers:
48 Hours

Chameleon

Fogarty

Ring – Ring (Novella)

Remnants of Deceit

Follow the Leader (Novella)
- *sequel to Remnants of Deceit*

Fall Out (short story) 2022
-*prequel to When the Hammer Falls*

When The Hammer Falls 2023

The Emirate of Dubai Thrillers:
Shadow of the Burj

Lure of the Falcon

Stand Alone Books:
Final Whistle (Soccer based thriller)

American Shorts (Editor and contributor)

The Girl Who Woke Up Speaking Mandarin (Short Story)

Zero Days Without Incident (RixFlix Short Story 1)

The Hoogflpaff Enigma (RixFlix Short Story 2)

Don't Go Alone (RixFlix Short Story 3)

Murder at the Raven's Claw (RixFlix Christmas Short Story 4)

The Platinum Stiletto (Royal Short Story)

Shire of Wessex Thrillers
Folly of Youth (Short story)

The Confessor (Short Story)